For Ruth,
with immeasurable
love,
T.H.

VENUS
in the afternoon

Previous Winners of the Katherine Anne Porter Prize
in Short Fiction

Laura Kopchick, series editor
Barbara Rodman, founding editor

The Stuntman's Daughter by Alice Blanchard
Rick DeMarinis, Judge

Here Comes the Roar by Dave Shaw
Marly Swick, Judge

Let's Do by Rebecca Meacham
Jonis Agee, Judge

What Are You Afraid Of? by Michael Hyde
Sharon Oard Warner, Judge

Body Language by Kelly Magee
Dan Chaon, Judge

Wonderful Girl by Aimee La Brie
Bill Roorbach, Judge

Last Known Position by James Mathews
Tom Franklin, Judge

Irish Girl by Tim Johnston
Janet Peery, Judge

A Bright Soothing Noise by Peter Brown
Josip Novakovich, Judge

Out of Time by Geoff Schmidt
Ben Marcus, Judge

VENUS
in the afternoon
Stories

by
Tehila Lieberman

2012 WINNER, KATHERINE ANNE PORTER PRIZE IN SHORT FICTION

University of North Texas Press
Denton, Texas

10 9 8 7 6 5 4 3 2 1

Permissions:
University of North Texas Press
1155 Union Circle #311336
Denton, TX 76203-5017

The paper used in this book meets the minimum requirements of the American National Standard for Permanence of Paper for Printed Library Materials, z39.48.1984. Binding materials have been chosen for durability.

Library of Congress Cataloging-in-Publication Data

Lieberman, Tehila, 1956–
    Venus in the afternoon : stories / by Tehila Lieberman.—1st ed.
        p. cm.—(Number 11 in the Katherine Anne Porter Prize in Short Fiction series)
    2012 Winner, Katherine Anne Porter Prize in Short Fiction
    ISBN 978-1-57441-466-0 (pbk. : alk. paper)
    ISBN 978-1-57441-477-6 (ebook)
    1. Jews—Fiction. 2. City dwellers—Fiction. I. Title. II. Series: Katherine Anne Porter Prize in Short Fiction series ; no. 11.
    PS3612.I33523V46 2012
    813'.6—dc23
                                        2012025399

Venus in the Afternoon is Number 11 in the Katherine Anne Porter Prize in Short Fiction Series.

This is a work of fiction. Any resemblance to actual events or establishments or to persons living or dead is unintentional.

Text design by Carol Sawyer/Rose Design

For Bati and Amir

". . . whittling and refashioning her so she could tell
how we are breakable and mortal, how
suffering is a grace and pain a living pearl. . . ."

—JOHN F. DEANE, FROM *OUT OF A WALLED GARDEN:*
THÉRÈSE OF LISIEUX

Contents

Acknowledgments

I would like to thank the editors of the journals where versions of the following stories first appeared:

Cutthroat: "The Way I See It"

Colorado Review: "Reinventing Olivia"

Salamander: "Cul de Sac" and "Into the Atacama"

Nimrod: "Waltz on East 6th Street"

Literal Latte: "Flammable Vacations"

Words and Images: "Fault Lines"

Side Show: Tales for the Imagination: "Anya's Angel"

As well as Dan Jaffe, editor of *With Signs and Wonders, an International Anthology of Jewish Fabulist Fiction*, which included "Anya's Angel."

As the stories in this book were written over a span of years, there are many people whose feedback, support, humor and love contributed immensely.

Much thanks to all of the members of my past and current writing groups—the original group: Dan Boyne, George Harrar and Joan Leegant; my Thursday night group: Pagan Kennedy, Susan Mahler, Karen Propp, Lauren Slater, Priscilla Sneff; the Thursday night offshoot group: Susan Dworkin, Karen Propp, Jean Trounstine; the longstanding Sunday group: Cathy Armer, Kari Bodnarchuk, Peter Brown, Laurie Covens, Bob Dall, Bill Ellet, Sara Fraser, Lucy McCauley and Lisa Perkins; my Writers' Room group: Jenny Barber, Pam Bernard, C. D. Collins, Linda Cutting and Carol Dine. My most recent group: Karen Propp and Susan Schnur. And to Andrea Oseas, who read and provided feedback on many earlier drafts of these stories.

I am very thankful to Jean-Dany Joachim for his many invitations to read.

I am grateful to Howard Wright for much needed help regarding window washing equipment; to Lynn Shirey and Ricardo Maldonado for Spanish vernacular; to Clark Vandervelde for his help with Dutch words and references; to Charles Bambach for German usage and verifying philosophical references; and to my beloved goddaughter, Sara Bakker, for medical verification.

I am enormously thankful to the Brownings for the peace at Wellspring House—a haven and a refuge. Also, to the Writers' Room of Boston, my in-town writing home for many years.

Special thanks to Miroslav Pinkov, Laura Kopchick and the readers for the Katherine Anne Porter Award, and to Karen DeVinney and Paula Oates of the University of North Texas Press.

For her brilliant eye and assistance in finding the cover art, Michaela Sullivan.

For her inspired cover design, Jane Winsor.

For their incomparable and priceless reads and suggestions and their deep friendship, Diana Brecher, Carol Dine, Karen Propp and David Wildman.

For their ongoing love and presence through the many years of work, Laurie Covens, Randye Friedrichs, Harriet Frost, Isabelle Guetta, Lucy McCauley, Andrea Oseas and Debbie Shapiro.

I am profoundly grateful to David Wilson for his love and support, and to Caitlyn, Abby and Garrett Wilson for opening their home to me and helping to create such a magical writing space.

And finally, to Amir and Bati, whose love and accompaniment are everything.

The Way I See It

"Death should be like losin your grip," I says. "No different than losin your grip and swingin into one of your windows—only it ain't a window and you sail right through to the other side."

There was four of us lined up in a row at O'Malleys. Healy with his usual pint, McKinney with his fancy scotch and soda, Sweeney suckin down a gin.

"Jesus, Mary and Joseph, will you listen to him?" Sweeney says, "from one day to the next gone loopers on us."

"Go to hell," I says. Loopers was not a word we used lightly. Mostly we saved it for the women—my woman in her day, God rest her soul, Healy's woman, whichever woman was goin through the change.

"It's the pint talkin," McKinney says.

"Nah," Healy pipes in. "Too much time in Cambridge. That's what I think. It's in the air."

McKinney spins around to face me. His gut's gettin bigger by the week and we're all thinkin if he don't watch it, he's headin for a coronary. "So Sutherland," he drawls. "Whatcha got for us this week?"

I look up at the TV where the Sox look beaten before they start.

"Sorry boys, nothin today."

"C'mon. Don't hold out on us. What's he been up to this week? Any handcuffs? Any fuckin faggots?"

"Dirty minds, all of you," I says. "Filth."

"Well," Healy says, "where the hell do we get it?"

"Well, I wouldn't say I have much choice, but man, you guys just roll around in it."

✿ ✿ ✿

It's too bad you can't confess another man's sins or I would do it, get on my knees in front of Father O'Conner and spill the litany of sins my eyes been forced to see. His hair would go white on me right then and there. I don't tell him because he might tell me to change jobs, tell me this is how the Lord is puttin temptation in my path, but what does he know really? And anyway, there's nothin like seein another man's ugliest secrets to make you understand in your bones what it means—sins of the flesh.

You know, when the girls were little, they used to have this doll house. Not one of those fancy ones that costs a hundred bucks and comes with furniture nicer than what you've got in your house, but one that my brother Tim nailed together for them one Christmas. Maggie had sewed curtains for the tiny windows, made furniture for the rooms out of wooden match boxes. And Katie—the one we always had to pull down from her dreamin like a helium balloon—Katie says one day that the rooms weren't really rooms but worlds. A whole bunch of different worlds smack up against each other, only no one knew it. And the dolls in the bedroom had no idea about the dolls in the kitchen, and that when she looked at all of them workin away in their little cubes of space, she felt like God lookin in on his creation.

Well I sure don't feel like God but when I'm rappellin down from window to window, it's like I'm seein snapshots—movin snapshots of these little worlds—each one deaf, dumb and blind to the other.

Mostly it's the usual stuff, but man—when you're just tryin to make an honest livin cleanin the next man's windows—there's a hell of a lot of grime you get to see. Grime that no ammonia is goin to clean up. The underbelly of the workin world—that's what we're given just when we're mindin our own business.

It's high on the tenth floor—the smut room. That's what I call it because what I've seen in there would make any decent man's skin crawl. The truth is this guy makes me sick. You can see that he thinks he's God's gift to humanity, the way he struts around like a cock in a hen yard. Women are his weeknight thing, but it was when they had us do the once over on the Saturday before inspection that I learned that his weekend taste was for boys. The kind you see in those underwear ads, all puffed up and lookin like they just stole their daddy's car.

When I'd come home on those nights, the woman would somehow know he'd been at it. Just as I'd be comin in, she'd reach across the couch and pick up her rosary, like I was the devil himself walkin through the door.

I made the mistake of confessin one night and one ale too many to the boys, told them what I'd seen, the whole kit and caboodle.

"And the desk," I was sayin, "Always the desk! What is it with these guys? Would he lose it if it were a bed? What in hell's name is wrong with a bed in the privacy of his house for Christ's sake?"

"What if you ratted?" Healy says then. "What if his company knew how he was usin their office? Their furniture for fuck's sake?"

"You should come down to the wharf," McKinney says, "Switch to our job. Whole building's empty."

Sweeney never says much, but now he says, "You know word is you could have supervisor if you want it. Nobody's got your seniority and don't fool yourself, they ain't gonna keep you up there much longer."

❁ ❁ ❁

Okay, so I'm stubborn. Is that such a bad thing? I know I'm pushin things but I don't want no desk job. Might as well pack me up and ship me off to an old age home where you lose your muscles, and then you lose your mind and then they turn you from side to side till you croak. As it stands now, the muscles ain't so bad. A few Advil with breakfast and I can mostly ignore the shoulders and back when they start their screechin.

The boss leaves me alone. Tells me soon the union's gonna put their foot down but since Maggie died, they don't want to ruffle my feathers. But that might all change after today. Because wouldn't you know it, just before lunch, a rag gets caught in the belay device and I go and get stuck. The belay jams just as the rest of the guys are leavin for lunch and I'm yellin like a lunatic, tryin to get them to hear me before they're too far. But they keep on walkin, not hearin a thing. The guys told me years ago to leave the higher jobs for the young kids we were breakin in, but I was stubborn.

The thing is with no obvious way down and me swingin like a hammock, I was scared. It's funny how even when you think there's nothin more anchorin you to this life, there it is, like a rumblin in your belly and you wantin more. Even with the woman gone and my nights a long stretch of beer and TV, there I was, wantin more.

And where do you think I was?—right by his office, only I look in and he's gone. The office is empty, just a few things on the desk I don't recognize, and then she comes in, this young girl and I think, no, it can't be and no, it isn't but Jesus, does she look like Bangs and for a moment I feel like it's Bangs who went and died on me and not just the woman. But of course Bangs never died. Just marched out of our lives like a freakin majorette.

It's not necessarily that the girl looked like Bangs, though they each have those freckles that make em look like a kid, but there was somethin else—an expression—a determined little look. Bangs's was harsher—had that hard, don't-get-in-my-way attitude like I seen in those girl sprinters in the Olympics. In your face, if you know what I mean. I can still see it—Bangs balanced on the top of the stairs ready to take them on a skateboard, Bangs cuttin her hair like a boy's and talkin her way onto the scruffy soccer team the boys had gotten together down the street. Bangs in eighth grade, snippin the front of her hair off so that the old lady and I would stop callin her that.

"Mary Beth," she said as she turned to face us, her bangs gone, the rest of her hair hittin her cheeks like Francis of Assisi.

"Mary Beth," as if we didn't know her name.

In the same tone that a few weeks later, I heard her talkin to her mirror, not knowin I was passin in the hall. "I'm getting out of here," she said to herself and she did. One day at breakfast she laid out brochures to some fancy girls' school she'd already applied to. Marched right out of Southie to this boarding school in Connecticut where she'd got herself a full scholarship, and then to Princeton which she said was pretty fancy as far as colleges went.

"It's in New Jersey," I'd said. "If I know anything, it's that there ain't nothin fancy in New Jersey."

◊ ◊ ◊

She's ashamed of me and that's the truth, and other than when the woman was dyin, I ain't seen hide or hair of her in over a year.

So there I am, stuck outside the girl's window, blowin this way and that like a plastic bag caught in a tree and she comes right up to the window. I raise my hands as if to say "What can I do?" and the girl smiles the kindest smile and puts a sticky note up to the window that says "just hang in there" and we both laugh and I tell you she was like sunshine after the flood only it was bittersweet kind of, because she was gettin this pain goin in me that I'd thought I was done with.

The next few times I cleaned she would wave to me, but she'd got busy. I could tell from the way they looked at her—the guys comin into her office—like she had their respect and all, and I thought, good for you, girl. That's just great and I thought she deserved it—though I knew nothin about her except that she got me missin Bangs all of a sudden, and Maggie, God rest her soul.

When I drag myself to church, there's one hymn that gets to me. The rest I could sleep through: Father O'Conner's sermons about the lamb and the pasture, about the water and the wine and the blood, and a million and one meanings of the trinity— that stuff's never done nothin for me. And I don't think it needs to be all that complicated. It's us idiots that go and complicate it, lookin to show that we know better than anyone else what things mean. They mean what they mean. Ain't that obvious? I mean there's God, his son and the Holy Ghost. What's the problem with that? Anybody got a problem with that?

But there's this one hymn, it goes "Gather Me, Gather Me Home" that gets me all choked up as if Maggie had planted those words in my day to make me remember, because, if I'm honest with myself, in our early days that's how she made me feel, and even later after all the spats and bad times, somehow Maggie made things right and without her it's like I'm a boat that's tippin and everything's slidin this way and that.

Sometimes I think she's watchin me. I feel it or else I'm losin some screws, which is what the boys would say. I can't even take out the magazines anymore without feelin guilty, and when Suzanne down at O'Malley's leans over the bar and her breasts are bare down to the very end—and she's got this killer rack—I look away. Can you believe it? When I was younger and the woman was around, I was no such kind of shy. I mean other than that early kettle of fish I got goin over that wait-ress in Gloucester when the kids were still little, it was only thoughts; never again did anything—too loyal when you get right down to it, and after that one, too scared. And I knew that Maggie had taken me back once but wasn't goin to be a fool for it twice. And the truth is I loved her. If I didn't know it before things blew up with that silly waitress, I knew it right when they did, Maggie packin herself and all the kids and I was like a man watchin his fortune sinkin. So after that, I was good. And in the end, it was only Maggie I wanted to wake up to anyway. Only Maggie I wanted to sit down and eat with, share a laugh with, grow old.

But we didn't get to grow old, did we?

That's mine to do and she left no instructions for that and the kids are crazy busy and I'm gonna go nuts if I don't figure out how to live without her.

✧ ✧ ✧

Six more months, they're tellin me, and it's a desk job for me, or if I want it, early retirement. In the morning, I hang for a few minutes before I start, just watchin the birds landin on the rooftops and terraces as if they were the tallest trees in some forest, the world sparklin clean at this height and free from all the sweat and work and also from its prancin, tryin to be this or that. Up here it all just is.

When I rappel down to her window, no, I'm not imagining it, the girl's pregnant. Looks like she must have been pregnant all along and I never noticed it, cause her belly's popped like an umbrella opening and she's breakin my heart because it's like seein Bangs pregnant, gone all soft and pretty. Thirty-seven now and Bangs and her husband doin their research into god knows what, doin their travelin and thinkin that they can just order a kid when they want, like from one of them freakin catalogues. But go try and tell Bangs anything. Maggie tried before she died and just barely had the time, the diagnosis made so late and all and Bangs not knowin for the first few weeks we knew.

We was wonderin why she never turned up and it was only later that Katie, of all people, says, "you sure she knows?" and Maggie has me callin the rest of them—Joey, Kevin, Chrissie and the twins. "You're kiddin," I says, my blood rushin to my head and poundin there like a fuckin drum. "No one's called Bangs? What the fuck is wrong with this family?"

When Bangs finally arrived, you could almost see her skin crawl around all the crosses and rosaries Maggie had around the bed.

"Hi, Ma," she said, and it was so strange. There was no Southie left in her at all. Just Maggie's face in this short, cute haircut like that actress that went and had that orgasm in the middle of a restaurant—but it's like she came from somewhere else entirely.

✲ ✲ ✲

Second time in a month, she doesn't even notice me. I'm doin her window slow, like I got all the time in the world, waitin for her to turn around and give me that first day of spring smile. I did the top floors fast so my time is good and we're havin one of those Indian summer days that gets you all confused about what month it is. And what I'm thinkin is that if I were this girl's father, I would be tellin her no girl should have to work so hard. I would remind her that even in this here city, certain days there's sun everywhere, bouncin off the buildings, swimmin on the water like a sparklin school of fish. That she should go and jog like the other women her age along the Charles, or strap on those roller blade things and be a kid again. They've given her too much to do and she's gettin older by the week, if my eyes are tellin me the truth.

✧ ✧ ✧

"Enough," Chrissie says when she comes over on Saturday. "Enough, Pop. We've got to start packing this stuff up." She hands me three books wrapped in plastic. Library books. Fuckin library books Maggie'd taken out just a couple of months before she died. And without expectin it, it gets me all shook up. More than the other things—her hair clips and stockings. "Why don't you take these over, Pop, when you have a chance."

"I will," I says. But I sit down to read them first. And it's one strange thing, how readin them I suddenly feel closer to Maggie, like I've turned back time and joined her where she went in her mind those last few months, even when we were all payin attention to her dyin.

When I finally take them back, I go up to the librarian and I says, "Can you tell me what Maggie—that's my wife— what she took out?" And she looks at me all polite, callin me

"Sir" and all and she asks me whether I'm meanin this month, this year, the last ten years—because that's as far as she's got records. "How about this year," I says and she taps somethin into the computer.

So I begin to read some of the books Maggie'd read, startin with the most recent and goin backwards. And it's like I'm holdin on to a part of her, joinin her in some secret place, though I can't tell her any of this.

And then, suddenly I get it. That where Bangs went was not about bein high falutin. It wasn't really about gettin away from us. Bangs had fallen in love with this—this funny other life you get to carry around in your head while you're goin about livin yours. The way you can see the whole world and ask yourself a million questions that never would have occurred to you without even leavin your front porch.

Maggie had some learnin. Her folks were dirt poor when they came over, but they hadn't always been. My own mother had pointed it out to me when I started courtin her. "Another class of folk," she'd said. "She'll always look down her nose at you." But Maggie never did. She never lorded it over me, but she also didn't think to tell me where she went when she sat there with her pile of books.

❁ ❁ ❁

Three weeks now and the girl's office has been dark. I hope she's takin a good vacation, lyin on a beach somewhere, her belly in the sun, with that husband that should be takin better care of her. Maybe, I think, she's on some religious retreat. There's a new large red Buddha in the center of her desk and next to it a sign that says, "Daily: The Dharma." And I don't know what the hell that means, sounds like somethin you'd eat over on the Greek side of town, but that can't be right. Instead the word sticks to me like it wants attention and in my mind, that's what I name her—"Dharma."

Then late in the winter she's back, or some version of her. It's like someone slicin open my gut, just takin a knife and havin a holiday with me because when she walks in, she's got the chemo scarf on and her belly is as flat as a pancake. Truth is somehow I knew it. The girl's color gone to ash just like Maggie's. I can see it sometimes now—death—snuck up behind someone like a friggin shadow. And there it was suckin the light from the room. What I don't get is why some of us get called early and others of us who seem no more deservin slosh through day after day. And to tell you the truth, I don't think that Father O'Conner or the Bishop or the Cardinal for that matter have come up with a good answer to that—God's plan and God actin in mysterious ways and all that. It's a load of crap. Truth is when you strip away the incense and the vestments and the Hail Marys, no one knows. That's why they have us prayin and confessin all the time. Like puttin your chips down all over the board, increasin your odds. But it seems to me it's a bit like lightning—kinda unpredictable and cruel and leavin no explanation behind.

You could tell in those early months, her belly still leadin as she came into her office that she didn't know nothin yet. Makin her lists, makin her calls. Always at the computer and on the phone, all day long. Don't know what she does but she does it for hours with that determined little look that makes me think of Bangs.

✿ ✿ ✿

Here's the thing. I don't really know Bangs. If the truth be told, I know more about this here girl in the big office than I could tell you about my own daughter. The woman knew this early on. "You've got to try harder, Mac," she'd say. "Bowling's not her thing. Take her to a play, to a museum." But museums always gave me the itch. From their "ain't we grand" halls to the way people tiptoe and whisper. Some of the paintings are okay if you go for little boys in ruffles and some long-ago high-flyin life, but they never did nothin for me. Except for one—the *Battle of Waterloo*. Now there's a painting. You could see the sweat comin off those horses—their bellies in their eyes, they was so scared. Men fierce and stupid, horses rearin like they's the ones with the sense.

Bangs yanked on my sleeve, pulled me away, "Daddy," she whined, rollin her eyes, "that's boring."

Boring! Like the portrait of someone's mistress all done up like the queen was the cat's pajamas. But that's what she liked and would make me stand in front of it for a million hours. And she would say, "She's so sad. Why do you think she's so sad, Daddy?" Then she'd make up some story. Somethin like because she was born speakin a secret language and there was no one in the whole world that could understand her and, I admit it, to me it was just a story she'd gone and fetched from that crazy imagination. It was only later, her room left with all her things exactly in place as if she wasn't goin to need none of it—and me standin there lookin around like an idiot that I got it—Good job, Einstein.

✷ ✷ ✷

I'll tell you the truth—because now with Maggie gone and Dharma fadin right in front of me like I needed any remindin—I know one thing and that is that we don't have the time we think we have. We go shufflin along in this life, fillin our bellies, puttin bread on the table, havin a laugh or two and then it's yanked away before we've made any sense of it. So here's the thing—I didn't do nothin to keep Bangs close after Maggie died. For a couple of weeks afterwards, she called me. If we didn't have nothin to talk about in person, over the phone it was just plain worse. I didn't look forward to those calls, and, truth be told, I went and let the machine get them one or two times. Then she stopped callin and instead of feelin better I felt like I had just dug another grave.

In the old days, before Maggie died, Bangs wasn't around much. She'd show up on Christmas like it was some kind of punishment. She'd come in and you could see she was glad, somehow, to see her brothers and sisters, and Maggie of course, but also itchy, uncomfortable. And she'd say, "How are you doing, Pa," and even with that sentence she somehow would make me feel stupid. And then I'd find myself gettin angry and Maggie would look like she was a buoy out at sea goin this way then that way with the conversation and I'd listen to Bangs describin to her sisters or brothers what she was doin— comparative literature. "Comparative bullshit," I'd say to Maggie. "What the hell kind of living is that?" and Maggie would look at me with those sad eyes like she was feelin sorry for me. "Now don't go and tell me you know whatever the hell that is."

❂ ❂ ❂

St. Pattie's Day and I'm not feelin so great. Every bit of me hurtin like my body's gone and decided to grow old overnight, and me wanderin from room to room, as if I'm goin to turn somebody up by lookin.

Never did that before, just walk from room to room like that. The woman kept their rooms the way they once was—a fuckin museum of child rearin. Even the rooms we'd gone and changed into somethin else still feel like their bedrooms.

❂ ❂ ❂

There's talk of a strike. Healy's in the middle of it tryin to get me involved. A few years ago I might have gotten all fired up, but the truth is I don't need more than I've got and I'm just settlin into this new life and the quiet of this house that I should move out of one of these days. Sweeney says I can fix it up real nice, paint it some new yuppie color so it looks like someone's summer house, but in the city, and a buy a retirement in Vegas, if I want.

✿ ✿ ✿

Monday morning and suddenly I'm feelin nervous, checkin the ropes, inspectin the rack. Had a bad feelin from the moment I woke up. I'm supposed to start on the twelfth but I lower myself right away to her floor. It's dark and the door is closed and her desk is just sittin there with the little Dharma sign and the laughin Buddha. And someone's left a fresh bunch of flowers. Don't mean nothin, I say to myself. Just someone wishin her well.

But the next time, the whole office is filled with flowers. The door is open and people are comin in and leavin notes and things. Once or twice, I seen the women start to cry. And there I am sobbin up at 100 feet, apologizin to Dharma like she can hear me. "Couldn't get to the funeral," I'm sayin over and over like an idiot. "Didn't know where the funeral was." You know, it's not hard to tell who's a good sort and who just ain't. You can see it on people like the clothes on their bodies. McKinney, who's always makin fun of his hippie kid who's into all this New Age stuff says that's called an aura but I say whatever the hell it's called, it's plain as day. We know who's in front of us, who we can trust, who we better not, and this girl was just as good as it comes, and the earth went and swallowed her anyway.

✿ ✿ ✿

The phone's ringin. They're meetin down at the Dubliner tonight at eight o'clock. They're telling me early so I can't make no excuse. "Don't be a spoil sport," McKinney yells into my machine. "Get yer ass down here. We'll be waitin for you."

But instead I pack myself a sandwich. Make a thermos of coffee. I pull into Sal's and while he's fillin my tank, I take out the old crumpled map we used to use on all our trips, and with my finger, follow the road across two states to where I'll find Bangs's house.

I drive past it twice before I finally find it, a small sign stuck into a mulberry bush, and then a long driveway. Bangs's house is one of those modern things that looks strange from the first second you see it to the last. Both sides of the house are glass and the front juts out in these concrete slabs that could be porches. Not my taste. Like some office building that went and had a nervous breakdown.

I'm not there two minutes, just standin a bit to the side tryin to summon the nerve to ring the bell, when the rain starts comin down in big fat drops so that it seems to me that the woman herself has gone melodramatic on me and is startin to cry all over both of us. Like the woman is just cryin and cryin.

And all that glass is good for somethin because I can see that Bangs has got a party goin. The women—I swear almost every one of them—in little black dresses. The men, a bunch of talkin heads from what I can see, not even noticin the women, and I look down at my worn corduroys, and I don't know, maybe it's the wrong day. And there's Bangs lookin so beautiful. She's all done up in this black dress and her hair's in some complicated set of knots and for a few minutes I think I'm gonna knock on the door, but instead I get back into the car and reverse down the driveway and turn onto the road. And as the car starts speedin up, I feel so light, like any minute I'm gonna rise out of the car like a balloon sailin up to the sky. Because the one thing that was clear to me through all that rain and glass was that death was nowhere in sight, not inchin up on her, or hidin just behind her like a shadow. It was nowhere near her. Not even close.

Reinventing Olivia

As soon as I woke up, I could tell that Olivia was already gone. The smell of freshly ground Sumatra was only barely discernible. There was none of the tight rustle of the *Wall Street Journal* that reached me most mornings from the kitchen. There was only the rising hum of my own anxiety as I realized that today marked the end of the summer in which I was supposed to have finished my novel. That I would need to place that dreaded call to my agent, and then at night, begin teaching my fall adult ed class, which was, my advance long since spent, my only current income.

Olivia had left me some coffee. The *Journal* sat plucked and plundered on the table. I should remind myself to include it in the growing list of items I wanted to ban from the house along with that new dialect, "corporatespeak," she was beginning to spout.

I threw on some clothes and walked the two blocks to the café where I usually did my writing. The walls, previously old chipped brick, had been knocked out to accommodate floor-to-ceiling glass so that it wasn't clear whether one was within or without, object or voyeur. The inside had been done up in bright blues and oranges, its piping exposed, its modern industrial look startled by its own offerings—the folds of rich cakes and pastries piled on every surface, still redolent in their woven baskets, in their carved African wooden bowls. The ovens—perhaps to also break down all divisions between creator and created—sat practically alongside the customers, now and then letting off a smell that transported you to an earlier time.

I came here practically every morning. I knew the other regulars by now, knew what they ate, what they drank. I had learned that there was a code. We must not speak to one another because we were all coming here for the illusion that we were unobserved. I had realized this one day, when unable to work, I'd sauntered over to one of them, a man about my age and said, "So what are you working on?"

"Jung," he said with a pained look, covering his manuscript with his hands. After that I kept to myself.

But I couldn't work at home. Olivia's stockings were everywhere. She left dresser drawers half open, bits of herself discarded in her search for the right look for the day. A lace shirt dripped on a chair, a discarded boot here, a high heel there. One would think that someone had had wild sex in this room, but it was only my wife rushing away from me. Swathed in silk, girded for conquest.

Conquest of what?

I could only imagine (and admittedly my imagination was febrile and yielding these days only where Olivia was concerned), that it was all aimed at the seduction of one Gustav Christianson, the rising star in her financial services firm whom she mentioned with that unmodulated tone that one reserves for someone one is attracted to. The day she had mentioned Gustav was the first time she had used the word *benchmark*. "At some point," she'd said, "we need to benchmark our relationship." She showed me some complicated charts from her office, hieroglyphic statistics, a document describing something called "function points."

"You must be kidding."

"Michael, I am just trying to help us."

That day I had gone to the local art store and bought a long roll of paper. *Benchmark*, I wrote, along with some of the other awful words she'd begun to bring home. I nailed it to the door of our apartment, to what had once been our sanctuary.

I took out a pad of paper, looked around for a few moments, then closed my eyes, tried to summon the world of Oliver, my protagonist. It was winter in New England in the present scene. A pristine snow falling after a week of such snow, no longer noticed for its beauty or the way it temporarily masked all mistakes and indiscretions but instead for its sense of entrapment. A world slowed so that it could not rush past itself, so that it had to stop and see.

And what did my poor Oliver see? I crawled into his room, entered the bed of his depression, the covers he kept shifting over this, then that part of his body, unable to get warm. I didn't know what he saw. That was the problem.

Oliver's wife, Marcela, had left him suddenly one day without any explanation, as if he should have expected it.

It was clear to her.

The detritus collecting.

The mold.

This was all the more of a betrayal because everything about Oliver had promised success. When Marcela had met him, he'd struck her as cerebral and worldly, a physical and intellectual nomad. He had degrees in physics and philosophy. He had lived all over the globe. She could see women look up when he entered a room, members of his department regarding him with respect, expecting great things from him. But somehow Oliver had gotten lost. He hadn't been able to make the concessions one needed to make for an academic life. He was not a political animal. And slowly, without a structure to hold them, the ideas he was juggling had grown less concrete. He could no longer play with them the way he once had, fling them in the air like so many glistening balls. They either shrank, collapsed on themselves, rolled around in his hand like opaque marbles, or came at him in some psychedelic state, large and looming, their edges running into one another. At the height of this, Marcela had left him. From the genius she had fallen in love with, the young maverick, the object of so much intellectual and corporeal lust that she could plot the minute they walked into a room, she began to imagine him suddenly an eccentric old man, undocumented, left behind, and her life by his side worn and difficult. She took the juicer, the microwave, all the gadgets he'd never learned to use and left.

For several months Oliver devoured women, or rather they devoured him. They clustered at his feet at parties as he discussed the space-time continuum. His mind was sexy. His face lost. Like Marcela, each woman he met seemed to think that somehow he had the missing answers, had his finger on some pulse. Until, one by one, he had all of their secret needs and desires strung around his neck. So many women he was expected to spring from their lives, so many days to lift from their torpor. He grew heavy with them and with the inevitable failure.

I wanted to rescue Oliver. Free him from the terrible stakes of his life. Help him stumble upon a world, a woman with whom he would come fully into himself. But for now I couldn't even get him out of bed.

All right, I thought. What about the physical scene? His room, his house? What would he see if he threw off the covers? What would he smell? What would he hear?

"Om shanti shanti Om."

No, that couldn't be right.

I spun around. Behind me two tables had been pushed together and eight orange-robed monks sat, eyes peacefully closed, practically lifting off the chairs, their coffee steaming and abandoned.

At the table just next to them, a woman unbuttoned her shirt, lifted a plump baby to her breast. To her left, an Indian woman stared out the window, graceful and shadowed, sadness hanging from her like so much gold. How was I supposed to work when life was presenting a more colorful pastiche than anything I could put on paper?

I gathered my things, trudged the few blocks home, dialed my agent and began to breathe again when after a few rings she didn't pick up. "I need another month," I whispered into her machine. Then I set the alarm for six o'clock so that I wouldn't miss my first class, pulled the covers back over my head and went to sleep.

✺ ✺ ✺

When I woke up, Olivia was tiptoeing around me in a short cream-colored slip.

"Pizarro," I said.

We called each other by revisions of our last names. When I had first done that she had protested that this was not her name, to which I had replied that the genius was in the revision. So from Olivia Parro, she had become Pizarro, and I, Michael Stamford, she at first had called *Statler* which had a nice New York ring to it, but lately once or twice she had called me *Stumped.*

I put my arms around her small waist as she was going past, pulled her onto the bed. She gasped.

"No, I'm already late. Tonight. I'll be back around eleven."

She bent down and kissed me on the mouth. It felt real. She was nervous and the kiss was as much to reassure herself as me. It was a critical dinner with some new prospect, she explained, pulling a dress I'd never seen from the closet. This was the biggest firm to ever flirt with a contract and it had been given to her to handle. The dress, black and very chic, ended way before her knees. I supposed this was a "power dress," and it was apparent to me exactly what power was being wielded here.

◊ ◊ ◊

That evening, I took a deep breath and pushed open the door to the corridor that held my classroom. I could tell the group that was going to be mine this fall semester by the looks of them, frumpy and blinking as if they'd just emerged from some collective cave. I knew all too well that at best, only one or two of them would follow through with what they now considered their life passion and that those two would run the risk of getting stuck, as I was, in the maze of the mid-life, mid-list author. That the bulk of them would not go the distance.

Did I feel sorry for them? Did I think they were wasting their time? Did I think about prodding them gently back into editing jobs, or social work or the degrees in psychology or literature they'd abandoned?

No, I had wrestled with all that and decided that it was better to feel passion, however misguided, than not to feel any at all. That it was not very different from falling in love. How many relationships yielded what one came to them for?

I scanned the room and played the game I often played with myself. Who would be the surprise talent? There was one woman who stood out from the large baggy sweaters, the abundance of black, the leggings and flowered skirts. She was in a crisp suit, the palest shade of yellow, her gold jewelry delicate across her neck. She looked like she had stepped out of a bank and from the short autobiographies offered up at the beginning of class, apparently she had. Her name was Yvette and she reminded me of Olivia. Would she be the one? No, somehow I couldn't make that leap. There was a young woman with blonde hair halfway down her back, eyes that looked old and wise, a child's face. I skipped over her quickly to look at the two men on either side of her who looked like they might sell insurance. I was about to settle on a housewife from Cape Cod when the door flew open and a biker with long, frayed gray hair and crossbones on a tattered leather jacket entered, and in a soft voice said, "Sorry I'm late." He placed his 280 pounds in the small chair next to Yvette and introduced himself as "Crash." It took me a while to recover from that entrance and from the realization that it might be Crash who would offer up poetry like from a dream, penumbral and mythical.

❁ ❁ ❁

She was going to be later than she had thought, Olivia announced from the machine when I got home. I opened the refrigerator. Nothing. Some wilting arugula, a bin of cheeses whose names I didn't know, a Nepalese hot sauce, yesterday's bread. I poured myself a glass of wine and turned on the evening news I'd recorded.

I didn't care about the news. I just wanted to see the child they featured for adoption in his Sunday best. The child whose difficulties were stated as though they were assets, the child to whom I would have offered a home if we had a home.

This was becoming a strange ritual. I couldn't remember now how or when it had begun. It was a bit like life, only condensed. One fell in love, imagined the places that would be filled. And then in a flash, the image gone.

My head began spinning from the wine and no food. I turned off the TV and crawled into bed. I told myself that I'd hear Olivia when she came in. I would hear her crisp zipper in the soft darkness. I would hear a foot slipping out of its shoe. I would feel her thigh under the covers. I took her pillow and held it to me for the few minutes before I passed out.

"Let's have a baby," I whispered to its soft flesh.

In the morning I woke to hear the door closing, Olivia's car starting up in the driveway. When I looked out the window, I caught only a streak of red flying around the corner.

✧ ✧ ✧

It hadn't always been like this. Olivia was going to paint and I was going to write. We were going to shun the seductions of accumulating too many things that would need to be fed with more things. We were going to have children and somehow clothe them and send them to the best of schools.

We were both then dealing in fiction.

We also had clearly not counted on how little I would earn. On watching our friends acquire degrees, houses, children, while our artistic careers crawled or stalled entirely. Or, perhaps more to the point, on Olivia's ability to walk away from herself, peddle her soul elsewhere.

✧ ✧ ✧

I pushed open the door to my study where the stories I needed to review for the next class were stacked on my desk. I usually waded through them in an arbitrary order but today, I tore through the pile, found Rachel Campbell, and started reading before I'd even pulled up my chair.

There was another game I usually played with myself the first night of class. It went like this: Who was the one I would lust after if I were single? And with whom (of course, if I weren't already in love) would I fall in love? For some reason I was sure that I had held back this time, that I hadn't done it. It had felt too possible, too dangerous. Still my eye had fallen twice on the young woman with long blonde hair and eyes that looked all too wise for her years. Rachel Campbell, she had introduced herself as they went around the room. She was here, she said, because she'd been working in isolation for too long. She didn't know where this would take her, but it was time to bring her stories to the light of day.

☼ ☼ ☼

Her story began with sex. Outside, the rough night of a Philadelphia street. Within, soft light, veiled music, the sprawl of cushions and pillows, all Middle East. There are low copper tables, Arabic tea pots. The young protagonist, taking in the room, stares at the pictures that adorn the walls, all of them of a village, sand-blown with turquoise domes and doors as the man who calls himself Mahmud lays her on her stomach, peels her clothes off like the skin of a fig, makes love to her silently. Moments later, she is panicking, the rough nap of the carpet under her cheek. She remembers the trot of the horses, sees a cluster of women, their heads bobbing in white bonnets above their dark frocks like froth on a night sea. She hears the prayers that were her first language, feels the field under her belly when secretly she had once lifted her dress to feel her skin against the rough earth.

So she is Amish! I read on. The young woman is spinning her history now. Her childhood, the books she secretly obtained through which she snuck glimpses of the world outside. The wagon ride to town to run some errands when she escapes to Philadelphia. This tall, olive-skinned man who approaches her on the grass of the university where she has begun to spend her days. They begin to look for each other between his classes. He wants to be an actor but is studying to become an engineer. Then the first bittersweet taste of sex. Her body a vessel for her own pleasure, a tool for her own torment. The discovery weeks later that she was pregnant. She wanders for hours on the sides of highways, a war of worlds raging within her. She walks and walks holding her belly like a cauldron. On a clear windless day she thinks she will explode.

✿ ✿ ✿

The next night in class, I found myself staring at Rachel. Where would her child grow up? The man, of course, would leave. He could not bring her back to Egypt. His family would have selected the daughter of friends years before he went off to get his prestigious degree abroad. That woman would be waiting for him shyly in the village.

In class I kept the discussion gentle. I made sure that Rachel knew that I appreciated the authenticity of the voice, the writing that still shone, daring and original, despite its rough edges. I watched her leave. The calm sway of her jeans, her hair so blonde it was almost white, parched corn, starched Sunday cotton. I watched her disappear into the night street and I wanted suddenly to follow, to protect her, hurry her into the armor she would need in her new life.

✿ ✿ ✿

Olivia was asleep when I arrived, the alarm clock set for four in the morning, airline tickets in the pouch of her open briefcase. "Last minute trip sprung on me—Chicago," the note on my pillow said. "Back Friday. Can you meet me downtown for lunch?"

"Of course," I told the note. "Of course," I whispered in her ear.

I went to the living room, poured myself some scotch and stood beside the bed. Where was she? Her body rose and fell with her breath. Her face was soft, her cheekbones momentarily hidden. Peering out from beneath the blanket, the relaxed flesh of an arm, a soft surrendered thigh. On the night stand next to her, all the mechanalia she would need for combat. I began to lift her gadgets and bring them closer, put them on the bed sheets around her, her cell phone by her sleeping hand, her car and house keys I positioned like earrings. The high-tech security cards that let her in and out of buildings I put near her curled hands, the alarm clock I put near her uterus. I didn't stop until she had a mechanical aura, until I had erased the softness she would not give me, the secret place she went to alone, the trail backward to who we had been, two lovers on a mattress in an empty room, our lives still undreamed.

There were women everywhere in my day, on the streets I walked down, in the café where once again I was trying to work, women with babies clinging to their shoulders or sucking for hours at their breasts right across from me. I saw the beginning of a breast, full and promising. I saw a chubby foot lift into the air in unadulterated bliss. I imagined Olivia at the airport, in the suite reserved for the Gold Club, crossing leg over long nyloned leg, opening a briefcase like it was Ali Baba's tomb, clicking on gadgets, returning the coffee for something stronger, her laptop emitting a slow, nuclear hum as she gently swivels in the soft leather chair and surveys the stock market.

I knew I needed to get back to Oliver, to take him toward that craved denouement, but all I could think about was women. The women around me, sipping their tea, their babies buried in the softness of their skin, women like Olivia escaping the mornings they had promised. Rachel, what were Rachel's mornings? I closed my eyes. Rachel in the morning would shake her nightmares from her like so many brambles. Turn like a sunflower toward the bright window, her long legs unsteady, another day of sprinting away from herself. She drinks tea in an empty white kitchen, bare feet on a tiled floor, a runaway from the hell of finding herself born into a world, which, it became clear all too early, was not hers. Rachel in the morning would arrive with relief to the sun dancing on the wall. The nights are full of demons waiting in ambush, waiting to pull her back into her former world, where she is expected to renounce her self-ish needs and accept being a stitch in that larger weave of the community, ever waiting to capture an image of god. Now she's falling freely in a random universe. Just before sleep, certain words return. Unexpected. Haunting. *Gelassenheit. Meidung.*

Rachel in my arms would thrash herself to sleep.

Rachel in my arms would learn the difference between bodies devoured like forbidden fruit on someone's floor, quickly, voraciously, almost without tasting, and the odyssey of falling through layer after layer of a person, discovering here a ledge to rest, there a peak to jump from.

Rachel in my life would give me a child, wild and lovely like the ones I collected weekly from the television, clinging to the foreign ground of my shoulder like an immigrant.

✿ ✿ ✿

I must have slept through the ringing phone but the machine brought me Olivia. I could hear an airport behind her. She was home, she said. She needed to go into the office to brief Brent on the trip but how about coming downtown like we had planned and meeting her at Fortuna's for lunch.

Yes, I thought, I would do it. I rarely ventured downtown. I barely left Cambridge where for better or for worse I could read everyone. I could guess the music they were listening to, how far they were on their spiritual search, whether they did Kundalini Yoga or Iyengar. But these people downtown, who were they?

✦ ✦ ✦

Olivia's legs were getting longer, I thought, as she approached me. No, I realized, it was her skirts that were shorter. It was gradual, subtle. Sex alluded to but just barely enough that it could be denied. Just yesterday, when I should have been writing, I was rummaging through the drawers and came across a picture of the two of us. Olivia's features were still soft, her body still rounded and welcoming. A body one could curl up to, temporarily safe.

When I met her in front of Fortuna's, she offered me her cheek. I chose her lips. "It's in the contract," I told her. I was pulling her closer to me, trying to imprint myself onto her linen suit.

She waited for me to finish, then stepped back and appraised me.

"How's your class?"

"More talented than usual."

She looked up surprised. "Oh good."

"Yeah."

"And how's Oliver?"

"He'll be fine." I could see the glimmer of a smile playing on her lips. We sat down, lost ourselves in the menus. Olivia ordered something complicated. "Same," I said and ordered some wine.

"Any interesting characters in the class?" she asked.

"Actually yes. There's a biker who writes poetic Sixties kind of stuff, a banker who reminds me of you."

"Go easy on her."

"And an Amish woman pregnant with a half-Arab child."

"What?"

Our food arrived and as Olivia began to eat, I told her the story. How unable to disappoint her family and the community, Rachel had undergone the baptism that initiated her into the Amish community of adults. Waiting for a sign, for that epiphanous embrace that would tell her that she had chosen correctly, dim her burgeoning fears, instead what arrives feels like death, the slow insidious death of her spirit. Then one day, almost without warning, she sees the moment dangling like an open door, and she leaps out of herself, out of her life, carrying on her soul all of the heartbreak she had left behind. The community of course voted to "shun" her, to excommunicate her from that point forward.

"Can you imagine?" I asked. "Can you imagine a family raising their daughter only to later discard her? How could anyone do such a thing?"

Olivia was looking at me as if from across a galaxy, her fork poised above the oriental chicken splayed like so many lotus petals on the blackened and fractured noodles.

"Did it ever occur to you that it might be fiction?" she asked.

"Nonsense."

She was silent.

"Just sleep with her," she said finally.

"What?"

"Just sleep with her. That's what this is about, isn't it?"

So it was that simple, was it? A commodity grabbed, a commodity taken. An appetite filled. Another day.

Or was she trying to goad me into the position of taking us over the edge so that we might finally roll apart, each to his or her own hell or salvation?

"Not so easy, Pizarro. Let me remind you about the gray areas where most of us live. That area in which somewhere you still love me, and I, you."

"Everything okay?" the waitress asked suddenly at my shoulder. We stared at her blankly.

"Fine," I said and ordered more wine. I suddenly wanted to get my wife drunk, derail this conversation before it got worse.

We were silent for a long time while we ate. When we stood up, Olivia a bit unsteady, I leaned over her shoulder and whispered, "I want to benchmark you."

She laughed. "You're not using the word correctly."

"I want to merge with you."

She smiled, looked at her watch. "Let's go home."

I was going to suggest somewhere else but she was right. Our apartment was much more exotic. As if we were cheating on our usual selves who barely saw one another, who created elaborate rituals in order to touch.

As soon as we were in the door, I lifted her shirt and put my mouth to her breast, eased the tight skirt over her hips, lowered her onto the oak floor like onto a deserted beach. Afterwards I almost had her laughing at herself.

There were moments when I could still hope.

But hope left me quickly. She had made love to me spectacularly and the more I thought about it, the more I found it disturbing. Had I, ironically, become the lover? The break in some other routine?

✿ ✿ ✿

"It's possible," my friend Russell was saying to me, over a beer that evening. "It's very possible."

Russell was like lighter fluid. Whatever fears I had, Russell took them and ignited them. It was a counterpoint to therapy to bring whatever I was going through to Russell. My therapist was always trying to escort me back to the parameters of the possible, show me how my imagination, my knack for story-telling helped me slip away from the feelings I needed to be feeling, a slick escape route I rode incognito away from myself. Russell fanned the flames.

"Where," he asked, "do you think they do it?"

I tried to picture Olivia's office that I'd been to only once or twice, the polished mahogany of her desk, the plush carpet.

"I really don't want to think about it," I said.

"All right." Russell was quiet for several moments.

The couch in the spare office? I wondered. The atrium up on the roof?

"Is there a roof?" Russell asked.

✦ ✦ ✦

Crash was beginning to look at Rachel, Rachel at Crash. I was becoming aware, as often happened, of the sexual energy in the class. The housewife from the Cape fluttered prose like from a romance novel. Yvette, the banker, whose tales betrayed a depth I had not anticipated, was definitely flashing her legs at me. No thank you. I had enough of that particular tease at home.

"Today we deal in tensions," I began. "The tension between the real text and the hidden text, the tension between . . ." I went on barely listening to myself. "We will start with Crash's draft of his short story, 'On a Night Ride Singing.'"

For a draft, it wasn't bad. Although punctuation was spare and sentences often ended with words either shooting off the page like sparks, or idling like a tired bike. Still it had its moments, landscapes dazzling as I imagined a biker might see them: the tunnel of sky hanging over an endless road, fields, pastures, barns, the small shrug of towns passed through in less than a minute, the dizzying lights of a city glimpsed in the distance. There was, of course, little discernible plot.

✿ ✿ ✿

I decided during that class that I was going to do it, finally take someone who deserved it and give her hope. Give her that little push of confidence she might need to go the distance. I was going to ask Rachel to join me for a coffee.

"You're playing with fire," Russell said. "Wait until after Olivia leaves you." His voice trailed off as he saw my face. "Sorry man, I thought it was obvious."

✿ ✿ ✿

The next night I stood in front of my closet. I owned nothing like those items in Olivia's wardrobe that said, "Take me, I'm yours." I threw on some jeans even though I was going to have to come home later to change. I had agreed to accompany Olivia to a corporate dinner at eight. I usually did my best to avoid her company dinners but she had said that it was important, that everyone was going to be there. Couldn't I please, just this once, come?

So I set up my coffee with Rachel for a couple of hours before I needed to be downtown so that I couldn't possibly follow her home. With Olivia's dinner ahead of me, I would have to remember who I was, where I was going in life in case the skin of Rachel's thigh brushed mine, in case those eyes that had seen centuries rush by looked invitingly into mine.

✿ ✿ ✿

We met at a noisy café, overrun with students.

"You have a very powerful voice," I told her as we sat down with our coffees.

"What?"

"Your voice—it's very strong, very unusual."

She smiled and I went on, telling her sincerely what I thought were the strengths of her work, mentioning some people in town she might want to study with, the areas of her work I thought could use a little more focus. I was aware that while what I was saying was sincere, I was also trying to be my most charming.

She took in everything, the gentle suggestions, the over-all encouragement, all the while fixing and tucking strands of rebellious hair beneath a bright paisley headband.

"I really appreciate this," she said, finishing her coffee in one long sip. She looked at her watch.

"You have to go?" I wasn't prepared for her to leave, to simply be here as my student, then rush back to her life.

"Yes, sorry. I didn't think we were going to meet for very long."

"I wanted to tell you," I said, standing up, "that I also truly admire your bravery, your courage in the face of what you've taken on." I tried to fight it, but my eyes lowered briefly to her belly.

She looked confused, and then she seemed to understand: "Professor Stamford, my story is fiction." Then she smiled, all of a sudden an utter stranger, a lovely young woman about whom I knew absolutely nothing. I started to apologize clumsily but was drowned out by the roar of a motorcycle pulling up outside.

"See you next week," she said, her hair swinging. I saw her climb onto the back of the bike and take off, her legs wrapped around Crash like around a continent.

✦ ✦ ✦

I went home, took a long, hot shower as if it could remove my stupidity. I put on my favorite shirt, some dress pants and a jacket and got into my car. I was halfway there when I looked down and suddenly remembered that Olivia loathed this shirt.

"Damn subconscious," I thought.

❀ ❀ ❀

Perhaps Oliver couldn't be saved. Perhaps that was what I was missing. Perhaps women would prey on him, the world would prey on him, pick him apart and then pass him by.

For a moment a specter of hope dances around him in the form of a young woman. He mistakes her attention for understanding, the ease he finally feels in her body with the ease he has not found in the world. But then, as that too dissolves, he begins to let go of his struggle for a place in the outer world. As he does, his work grows more faceted, complex. He begins to inhabit his world like a monk, relishing the withdrawal from his body. He doesn't see women as they pass him any more than he sees the bread that he eats hurriedly to quell his hunger so that he can arrive to his next thought. Marcela, passing him one day on the arm of her new husband, catches her breath, pauses. There is a beauty to his face, lit up like a holiday angel. For a moment something rises in her, a sadness, an old longing as big and melancholy as an abandoned house, but then the light changes and before Oliver can see her, she moves on.

❀ ❀ ❀

I pulled up to the posh restaurant where I was meeting Olivia. Even the valet who looked pained to have to park my car made it clear that he knew I didn't belong. I saw a cluster of the corporate wives in the lounge by the entrance and without making eye contact, I slid past them and into the bar. Olivia was perched on a high leather bar stool in a short black dress, sipping something pale, it seemed to me, without wetting her lips. She saw me, started to smile, then took in my shirt and bristled. *Okay*, she seemed to say, her eyes suddenly avoiding mine. *If this is what you want. If this is what you want, be very careful.* For a moment I thought I saw a tear forming.

They were coming toward us, the men, all lean with hard gym bodies and expensive suits, some of them so young, others with salt and pepper hair they'd let grow a bit long to hold onto a vestige of the hippie days they had left behind. I couldn't find anyone who looked like he might be Gustav.

"And what is it that you do Michael?" one of them asked me after Olivia had introduced us.

"I'm a writer."

"Wow. Would I be familiar with your work?"

"Michael's a novelist," Olivia interjected.

"Ah."

For a moment I thought I saw envy flit across one or two of the faces, but it was quickly gone. Instead I saw that what was dawning on them, since clearly my name was not associated with any blockbuster movies, were the financial implications for Olivia.

I had just sunk from corporate spouse to troubled early marriage that had not yet given itself up. I saw Olivia looking at me from the tall glass distance of a postmodern building. I saw that through the lens of these men, she could barely see me. That it was for this that she left me each day, from this that she returned to me.

"Which one is Gustav?" I whispered to Olivia.

"Gustav? Why? Gustav's not here yet."

Brent Murdoch, the CEO, was approaching, and practically on his arm, a tall blond god who must have been Gustav. Gustav looked as golden and untroubled as all my clichés about his country. He had the kind of face that looked innocent but could mask a Viking, long arms that could hang deferentially at his side, or lift Olivia easily, carry her away like willing bounty. The CEO looked a lot more his part with his horn-rimmed glasses, stylishly long hair, his yellow suspenders peeking out from under his suit, dark socks confident in Italian loafers. If he had not already slept with Olivia, he would, I thought. Perhaps in the penthouse suite of some hotel in the South of France where they went yearly for their little "Chairman's Club" to which the spouses were always officially invited but never came. It was clear that Gustav was the one to be neatly disposed of. Brent had looked me up and down and, in a corporate nanosecond, taken in the lack of connection between myself and Olivia and decided that I did not even require a strategy.

The wives entered, a bouquet of flowered dresses, and we were all ushered into an alcove drunk with lilies and the soft shadows of wealth. We sat down around a long oval table and Brent ordered wines I'd never heard of.

Under the table, I put my hand on Olivia's leg. The muscled thigh in its nylon shrunk back from me initially, then moved closer. Nuptial obligation?

The shrimp arrived on their skewers. The head of a rare mushroom was delivered on a small silver tray, marinated and sprinkled with herbs but nonetheless severed and primordial. The bread steamed when I broke it open.

"We are here," Brent began, "to celebrate this quarter's wonderful financials. And to congratulate Gustav Christianson and Olivia Parro on their extraordinary work and their joint promotions to the positions of Vice President."

I looked over at Olivia. Her smile was as restrained as the lighting, the muted presence of the waiters who must have been there given the disappearance of the crumbs I knew I had dropped. I did not see surprise. Only a quiet pride. No, the surprise was mine. Brent had no doubt lured her earlier into his office suite, uncorked some champagne from his private bar and handed her this gift himself, away from the prying eyes of her colleagues. He wouldn't have had to touch her. The power of what he was handing her and the smooth charm of his delivery would have been seduction enough. Now she sat here, favored concubine, avoiding me like a relative from the old country.

✹ ✹ ✹

I lay awake that night wondering how Olivia could be so far from me in our one bed, listening to the uneven rhythm of her breath and spinning a bunch of different endings to our story. The one I settled on went like this:

Olivia, wise woman that she is, comes to realize that if she crawls into Brent's net, she will be eaten alive. He has a wife and children, houses that spill onto acres of land. She keeps him circling, marveling at the clients she brings in, at the ways in which she continuously surpasses whatever goals he sets. Instead she chooses Gustav, and when his intuition, brazen and sharp, reveals an undiscovered opportunity in Scandinavia, she follows him there. Rachel and I have five children with hair the color of corn fields but who mysteriously love the urban canyons and crevices of the city. I complete my novel and it's a huge success. Though no one expected this, given its more literary bent, it somehow crosses over and is translated and serialized in many languages. Somehow, through some quirky act of fate, Gustav receives it from the international book club he's joined. Olivia, coming in the door of their blond wood and glass house notices it in the pile of mail. She lifts it, reads the praise on the back cover, learns of the prestigious prize it has won. She opens the book jacket to finally look me in the eye. What she sees is a man she could have loved. She tucks the book under her arm and slips out of the softly lit den where Gustav is on the phone in front of a pile of reports. She steps outside onto the patio and stares out for a long time at where the boundaries of her property begin to dissolve into the endless Swedish night.

☼ ☼ ☼

The real ending, of course, went like this. I had the apparently ridiculous idea—Russell wouldn't even sanction it by looking me in the eyes—of taking Olivia to Vermont for a weekend. I thought perhaps if I could catch her in the net of intimacy, set a mood that created the illusion of some new adventure, then gently I'd lure her back.

Did I really think it would work or did I want for one last time to lay my head between her breasts, drink in the rhythm of her sleep so that I might get to keep those softer, more habitable memories. I don't know and it doesn't much matter. Even the way it started should have warned me. We began by arguing over whose car to take. I finally suggested that we take neither but simply put them side by side and then push them over the edge of a cliff and see whose went flying down faster. Whose hit the bottom first.

"Not funny," she said.

Then she gave in. She stopped fighting. That too should have been a warning. I have to say it was lovely to see her in my '77 Citroen, with its frayed seats, its loyal soul, in the soft clothes she still sometimes wore on weekends—a tunic the color of sand, a flowing skirt, leggings like a dancer's, shoes that slipped easily off her feet. Her hair got looser and wilder as she lowered the window and we began to wind our way out of the city. We drove for a little over an hour in silence. As long as we were silent, I could somehow hope. It was getting dark when I noticed that we needed gas. I spotted the dim fluorescent lighting of a station up ahead. From the road, it had appeared open, but as soon as I pulled in and turned off the ignition, it became clear that it was not only completely closed, but abandoned.

"Well, we have enough to get us to another station," I said turning the key, but the car wouldn't start.

"Great," she said, staring ahead.

I popped the hood, jiggled the wires that I'd jiggled so many times before to bring my beloved car back to life. It produced a shudder, then what incontrovertibly sounded like a last gasp. It was hopeless, I knew, but I remained behind the hood, buying some time.

I had an emergency light. I would just put it on the side of the road and someone would get us towed. We weren't that far from the next town. Perhaps we could get there, find somewhere to rent a car. I didn't look at Olivia. Just got the light out of the trunk, put it by the side of the road, got back into the car.

"Terrific," she said. "Well I'm going to pee."

She opened the door, began to get out. At that moment, a dog appeared from behind the closed building, large and mangy, wild, black. He began to run toward Olivia. She closed the door quickly. He jumped up on the side of the car, barking madly.

She sat huddled against the door and I could see it clearly. She felt beaten to have her choices come down to me or the dog.

She wouldn't leave the car but I couldn't fool or flatter myself. She was leaning against the door with all her weight. She would not move a centimeter closer to me if she could help it.

I reached out a hand. She didn't take it.

"Lovely," I said. "One episode of impotence, and not even mine, damn it, the car's, and you are off."

"Michael don't do this to me. Don't write the script for me."

"Pizarro—I'm losing you."

"Michael—talk to me straight. How much longer?"

"How much longer what?"

"How much longer this treading water? This life?"

"What's wrong with this life? What life do you want?"

"The one we were supposed to have."

"The one you mean that would have included my brilliant success? Do you think that could make you happy? Is that what you want?"

"Perhaps if it included my freedom."

"Your freedom? You have your freedom. You're free to build your little dynasty and run it in your short black dresses, entrap with your savvy—is that the word?—the heart and mind of one Gustav Christianson. Free to close your womb to me. Free to return to me when it all gets a little too scary. Why are you still here?"

At that moment, I don't know what I was thinking but I leaned over and threw the door open. The dog rushed up to the door, barking ferociously. Olivia reached into the back seat, pulled out her small overnight bag and without the slightest hesitation, stepped out of the car. The dog circled her, bared his teeth and hissed. She stood very still, paler than I've ever seen her. She didn't move or scream, just stared at him with determined hatred. The dog growled a bit more softly, then ran off to the trees behind the station. She smoothed her skirt, wound a scarf around her neck and without so much as a glance at me, began walking calmly down the road.

"Pizarro," I shouted, but she was already turning a bend, disappearing into the New Hampshire night.

Cul de Sac

Alma

"So here's a secret from the future," Alma begins.

Samantha, halfway through her breakfast, rolls her eyes and slams her palms over her ears. The sunlight, sneaking past the bruised cactus plants lining the windowsill, glints off the stud in her nose and the hooks that dangle from her lip and brow.

"Mom, don't," she says, scrunching her eyes closed.

But Alma is on a roll.

"Nobody told me so I'm going to tell you because somebody should have told me."

"Mom, stop."

"It doesn't arrive. None of it arrives."

"Mom, for god's sake, stop it."

It is cruel, she knows. Where have her maternal instincts gone? The instinct that once made her leap between Samantha, wondrous, beautiful toddler and the bully in the sandbox about to run his truck's wheels through her hair. Now what she really wants to say is, *Those wheels will find you anyway and twist your hair until you have to cut it all off or go on living with one more man's plan gone awry.*

She turns and leaves the kitchen. This was what love she can mete out at this point—the act of removing herself.

"Morning," Darryl says. He passes her tentatively and sideways in the thin hallway between the kitchen and the back stairs. She doesn't answer; nor could she say what she felt in that second when his body flattened itself against the wall, when briefly it was right there, the smell of him, the vulnerable, sleep-troubled territory of his unshaven face, the boy-man she'd grown up with—although they'd met in their thirties, still, it was still as if they'd grown up together.

All she knows is she wants to be done with it. Won't he let her be done with it?

She makes her way to the front room where each morning she sips her coffee, looking out onto the neat lawns of their neighbors and the tangled mess that was hers and Darryl's. Every day, she has to pass the couch Darryl inhabits now like a country, his leather jacket hanging from one corner like a flag, a small overnight bag on the floor—as if in just an instant he'd be on his way.

For eight months he's been on his way, but still he's there, finding every last bit of her sanity, and like a sniper, fracturing it, bull's eye. Some nights he's gone. Some nights he's back so that each day is like a film reel playing over and over, only she is never inured to the pain of it. Each day she watches him leave her.

From where she sits, she hears him pouring his coffee, then the "fuck" as he takes a sip and scalds himself. She hears his footsteps begin in her direction, doubtless to ask her if it always has to be so fucking hot, but he stops and reconsiders. This is worse than anything, that he is no longer even game for a fight.

Then leave, she thinks.

Two nights ago he'd crawled in at four in the morning, three hours after she'd begun her pacing.

She had dreaded and hoped he was wrapped around a tree. When he came home, looking as bad off as she was and not smelling of anything but his own heartbreak, she went to the couch and swung a fist close to his face. She stopped and laughed, and shaking her head, began to cry, and he pulled her down into the valley of his body where they knew each other well. But in the morning, she awoke in her own bed—had she dreamt it all? A memory flitted up of waking on top of him in the middle of the night, her back aching, and reluctantly heading upstairs to her bed. No, she hadn't dreamt it. She threw off the covers then and hurried downstairs, to find, as she suspected she would, a couch stripped bare again, the cushions straightened as if they'd never been disturbed by the feat of it—hours of fucking—a whole marriage's worth of sex and desire. In those dim and stolen hours, they'd made their way back to the heady, intoxicated instincts of bodies that loved to play—as if once again they'd found themselves in the old inn they went to on their anniversaries, that low-ceilinged room from another century in Nantucket, the leaded glass spooned around a roiling sea, or in her office on a lunch break, after his affair. She had reacted to his affair a year ago by briefly trying to turn their marriage into one, as they advised in the magazines she read in waiting rooms. That had been the horror—that she'd found herself doing it—her thrill much darker than intended because of what she didn't tell him—that she knew, even then, in her clearest moments, there was no saving them.

✲ ✲ ✲

Samantha leaves the kitchen and drags herself upstairs. Alma knows that despite the early hour, her daughter will manage to be late for school again. Samantha was bearing the brunt of it all; her angry music and funereal clothes felt like a personal accusation at Alma for failing to keep her father moored and happy.

Alma pulls herself out of her chair and puts her mug in the kitchen sink. How will she make it through work today? The dim radiology room, her whole psyche tilted toward the screen, hoping against hope to see only the empty expanses of darkness filtering through the bones, organs that had not become more than themselves. What were the odds that the day would bring more good news than bad? She gives herself the same cheerleading speech she always has—even the bad news is good news if caught early—that yes, she is often the messenger, but her very act of discovery might shift the odds in the patient's favor. But on her difficult days, more than statistics should allow, she found tumors lined up on bones like beads on an abacus.

She doesn't know where Darryl has gone. Maybe he's stepped out into the yard to avoid her. Maybe he's downstairs in his studio. She doesn't know why he refuses to sleep there. She imagines it's to remain in her face. Yesterday morning when he came to pick up the clean shirt he'd forgotten and his dirty laundry (he didn't do his laundry at home anymore, which seemed to her the clearest sign there would be no return), she asked him point blank where he'd been. He looked her in the eye and said Lila was back in the hospital and that when he wasn't here, he was staying down the street with Max and sleeping in Lila's office, now a guest room. Would he lie about something like that?

Now she heads upstairs to get dressed. From the landing, she sees that Darryl has sprawled out on the couch again, his eyes closed. As Alma's steps creak on the old wooden stairs, she hears the door to Samantha's room click shut.

Lila

Lila decides to dream herself another life and walk into it as if into the painting that hangs on the wall in front of her and fills her entire view. She focuses on the painting so she won't see all the tubes and wires that tether her to this world. She imagines the taste of paint, the fan of sky. She wants to disappear into the painting, far from the foreground where an acre of wheat bends under the tongue of an invisible wind. The Victorian house that sits behind the wheat splits the landscape; there in front, a field with furrows, a scraggly sunflower bent the wrong way, and the house, all turrets and angles. It is impossible, Lila thinks, that admixture of sunlight and dusk, and she moves toward the dusk which holds the last of what is recognizable before a deep fathomless night. Somewhere she has a place there in that twinkling valley where she will hide until she wakes up in a different body. Every day she seeks the right image to still her mind. Every day, a different metaphor. Today the sun in the foreground warms her face, fills her with energy—has she ever moved so effortlessly?

But then her husband washes in on a wave of cheer and she is back in her hospital bed. How can she dare pierce it, his effort, his cabaret of stories? Today, Max tells her, Tyler threw up on top of the babysitter's head as she lifted him into the air, then giggled at feeling better, at the surprise on the adults' faces. Lila smiles, then realizes that Tyler might be sick and begins to panic—she starts to tell Max what to do and he stops her. He will figure it out. He goes on crowding the hour with stories. He fills her in on Darryl's adventures. At some point she will need him to stop; she will need him to really talk to her. But right now she lets him go on. How could he be capable of more right now? What prepares you for watching the person you love grow to resemble a daguerreotype? The sepia of earth and blood and shit, the white of bones, the tumors everywhere. She imagines the scans they refuse to show her tell the story of her body turning into stone.

Since the day of the diagnosis, when they'd both broken down, Lila hasn't seen Max cry. He's so determined to be a perfect hero, and it worries her. But how can she challenge it? What would she put in its place?

She shifts her attention back to what he is telling her about Darryl. Darryl, who once sat at their dining room table, smitten with his brilliant wife Alma. Darryl, the childlike, inexhaustible artist, not tamed but bewitched by the strong woman who moored him, who held things steady for him and for their beautiful, headstrong daughter. Darryl sleeps on the daybed now, in what had been her office. Lila imagines him keeping vigil over her drafting table, or playing with the adjustable triangles, the French curves, the X-Acto knife, architecting a new life. At first she protested, feeling a deep disloyalty to Alma, even if they were not as close as the men. This had been the first time she'd had to let go—take herself out of the equation. "Turn it into a guest room," she had said, then resisted saying "for now."

Max is talking and she turns her attention to him. In the middle of the night, he says, he suddenly heard, "What the fuck?" and something breaking. When Tyler started to cry, Max had gone to him in time to see a woman passing in the hall. In the morning, he gets the story. One of Darryl's women. She drank so much she mistook a sculpture on Lila's shelf for a lamp. Attempting to turn it on, she'd knocked it to the ground and fled. Darryl had combed the neighborhood for an hour before he found her on someone's front stairs and insisted on driving her home. And Lila knows suddenly that Max will no longer tell her any stories with happy endings. This is the harvest he will bring: for her, the absurdity of life.

What we have, she thinks: the foibles of others. Our own knowledge that we have not lost sight of each other, that we have not yet made a mess of things. There are worse states than dying while you are still in love.

Max

Tyler is crying and for a moment I'm grateful because I know now who I am, what I need to do; it's pulled me from the shore of this crazy-ass dream in which I'm flying over a beach—low as a seagull—about to land on a sand bar. The sand's glistening and the water's inching up higher and higher and there is nothing I need to do but dip my right wing just the slightest bit. It's so beautiful and the wind is on my face and I am about to touch the wet sand when I hear a baby crying and I remember I can't be here because I've forgotten the baby and the baby is crying only I'm too far away and I'm a bird. And I shake myself awake and look at the clock and it is five in the morning and Tyler is crying. As I'm walking to his room, Darryl comes in the front door with a woman with long red hair and a tiny skirt and we nod good morning and they walk past me. I wonder how he dares sneak women in with Alma just a turn of houses away but maybe the game is the point and he is begging to be caught.

I want to say to him: This is not the time, man—can you find another place? But also I am drunk with the lust filling these rooms. I am—it is so obvious as to be embarrassing—staying alive by way of his hunger and adventure.

I have to expand my previous notion of Darryl to include his new capacity, his appetites. It is useless to tell him that these women won't separate him from the parts of himself that still cling to Alma. At first I had to stop myself from talking to him about it. But now, a few weeks in, I refrain because I no longer believe my own drivel. Because I am beginning to want what he has—whole mouthfuls of life. I dream of flesh that glows, of a woman strung across my bed as in a painting.

Instead I go to the hospital and turn Lila from side to side to prevent bed sores. I hunker down and stroke her retreating flesh as if my whole life had prepared me for this. It is more awful than I imagined, the little indignities we grow unembarrassed by; it is more beautiful—her face at peace as the morphine kicks in—the morphine meant to mask the millions of gnats gnawing at her bones.

She looks out at me from the grave of her body and I see she pities me having to reckon with the detail and downright messiness of her departure. It is only when I turn her on her belly that I see a body I remember, the long back, the shoulder blades like delicate wings. From behind she is still Lila and I can even feel some crazy trace of desire. And then those terrible moments when she closes her eyes and the doctors invite me out into the hall.

This experimental treatment or the lesser-known, more aggressive one.

Pummel her or let her alone.

She and I never completed that conversation, nor the one about hospice. Who would have thought that we'd run out of time so quickly? Nothing in place, nothing ready.

"She has to decide," I tell the doctors.

✧ ✧ ✧

I come home to the sounds of sex. Darryl has found women who can escape their lives during the day—while Tyler is at day care—bartenders, librarians who work the night shift. They come to the door, timidly or brazenly in the hours both before and then safely after Tyler is asleep.

Darryl is a cliché. With all his talent, all that finds its way into those huge and extraordinary paintings, he can't think his way out of the obvious. Where will it end, this reckless, middle-aged joy ride? Is this what I would have become? I remember when we met him and Alma, and Samantha, who was only nine. They'd just moved into the final house on the cul de sac and, within a week, it was clear that like us, they forgot to tend to their grass until it was close to knee high. One day, I was coming back from a run by the pond and Darryl, his long curls streaked with gray, was sitting atop a used-looking John Deere mower that was sputtering and stalling on their overgrown front lawn. As I passed by, he looked up at me, and with a kid's smile, said, "Flummoxed, man. Fucking flummoxed." I helped him get it started again and a week later we all had dinner—so glad to have discovered each other, transplants from the city, here for reasons to do with ridiculous real estate prices and the illusion that we might cultivate sprawling, colorful gardens. And Darryl, Alma, and Samantha seemed to me then who we might become, a family still vibrant so many years later.

❂ ❂ ❂

More spent than usual, I drag myself into the kitchen and put up some coffee. Lila had been distraught all morning—a rare slip from the calm control of the last few months. Her panic hit harder than everything else—harder than the scars where her breasts had once been, the sallow color of her skin, the bones protruding from hips grown ancient and unknowable.

I hear a cluster of footsteps in the hall and the back door close. They have left. The guest room, again, a quiet theatre between acts. Ten minutes later, the doorbell rings. I am confused and more so when the open door frames a young woman. She is in jeans and a light pink T-shirt and a worn leather bag hangs lower than the bottom of her shirt. When she moves, the shirt lifts to show a strip of unmarred skin.

"Darryl isn't here," I tell her.

"Who is Darryl?" she says with a thick accent I recognize as Polish.

Then she says, "I am Alenka. I come to clean. Sadie sent me."

Sadie is a close friend of Lila's and it begins to make sense.

"She shouldn't have done that. I don't need. . . ."

"She told me to tell you that you need."

I lead her to the pantry and all the cleaning things in a large bucket. I find myself in one of Darryl's afternoons, my body crackling with sex, my mind begging for this respite. Am I imagining it or has her walk slowed, acquired a soft sway? We bend at the same moment to lift the bucket and our shoulders collide and she blushes. So I'm not wrong and I get there before her and lift the bucket, but once it's in my hands I have no idea what to do with it, so I take it into the den and she follows me. I don't need to look at her again because I have already memorized the lift of her breasts in the pink shirt, the collarbone that rises and falls as she breathes, the three glittering stones—pale green, turquoise, and teal blue—that crawl up her earlobe.

"Where would you like me to start?" she asks, and again I don't know if I can trust my own mind because there is a playful lilt and a half-smile tugging at her pretty little mouth. *Start with my eyes*, I want to say, *with my face, my hands, the inside of my palm.*

Instead I excuse myself to get the stroller ready for collecting Tyler from school. I throw together some diapers and juice boxes, his chewed and beloved Eeyore with its partially severed ear. I mumble something to her about just latching the door from the inside when she's done and I leave. I walk the few blocks to the day care center, then take Tyler to the park. While he throws sand in the air and laughs, I climb onto the thick slab of wood and fraying rope that hangs empty beside the bucket swings, and pump higher and higher until my mind whirs to a stop.

Alma

Alma slips into her office chair and dims the light, flicks on the screen. The first image looks like a bouquet of balloons, lilting to the left. There is only a second in which she can trick herself, see the image as anything other than what it is, a rounded atelectasis, a lung mass, virile and multiplying. She picks up the file: a fifty-six-year-old male shipyard worker who came into the outpatient clinic complaining of shortness of breath. Could be asbestos. She enters her interpretation and comments, is about to move the file to the Reviewed folder, but then she stops, opens it again, reads on. Married, two children, ten and thirteen. He will likely be gone within the year.

The next image fills the screen, the bottom ribs obscured by a cloudy mass. Above it, a granular, irregular whiteness. Left para-aortic mass. A thirty-nine-year-old female diagnosed with Hodgkin's Lymphoma. Two kids—two and four years old. Alma tries to look away from the file but she can't. Ever since she learned Lila was at Bedford Memorial across town, she can no longer maintain the dispassion critical to her sanity.

The next patient's scan stops her in her tracks. There is almost nothing left of the woman's organs that has not been

invaded. A forty-five-year-old female, one child—five years
old. Advanced metastatic breast cancer. Osteolytic metasta-
ses. Same as Lila. This scan to see whether the Abraxane has
had any success where the earlier chemo hadn't. She clicks
on one of the previous images, lines them up side by side on
the screen. The disease has not only resisted treatment, it has
continued to thrive. She turns away and then looks back at
the file. It is too late to assume her clinician stance. "Don't,"
she tells herself. But on her lunch hour, she takes herself to
the rooms of the two female patients. She can barely see the
Hodgkin's patient for the forest of flowers that has sprung up
around her bed. The woman is sleeping and Alma slips out
unseen. She takes comfort from the fact that the patient looks
strong. Judging from the flowers, she has a net of family or
friends or both.

But one floor down, the breast cancer patient brings her
no such comfort. The forty-five-year-old woman is wasted
away, her face chiseled and taut, as if the skull beneath the
skin was clamoring to surface. The room is full of the hush
of hospital death, its whirring, white-noise symphony around
the bed. Alma is standing in the doorway when she sees a
hive of doctors coming down the hall. She recognizes the
attending and they nod to each other, then she follows them
in. A woman—friend or relative—had just begun to read to
the patient from a notebook and stops as the doctors come in,
check charts, and leave. Only Alma doesn't leave.

"May I?" Alma asks, and pulls up a chair. She adds, "I am
her radiologist," as if that explains anything, and the woman
with the notebook nods.

Lila

She wakes up unsure of the time or day. In front of her, pure white. She summons the energy to turn her head to the wall. "Where is the painting?" she whispers to the nurse when she comes in.

"Oh they've taken 'em all down, hon. They're putting up some new art, if you call these art."

"I need it back," Lila says, the tears coming foolish and hot.

"I'll see what I can do."

Later, when Max comes in with Tyler in his arms, she wants to turn away; it hurts so much to see them. Cecile from her office arrives, armed with a gift basket of lotions and some books on tape which she can't imagine wanting to listen to.

They won't say it but she knows that the weeks no longer stretch like an empty desert road.

They all look at her as if she has the answers. She doesn't have the answers. She has to let go of the questions. Even as her body dissolves, and this is the feeling when the morphine kicks in, something in her is sharpening. Her mind drifts in and out with the painkillers, but she knows something she didn't know before and she is coming to it just as she is losing speech or the energy to speak. Within her is something vast and beautiful. Like an unseen ocean. She senses its lull and rhythm, she hears it if she listens carefully. But she's not ready yet.

She falls back asleep. When she wakes, Max and Tyler are gone and the painting of the house is there again. She notices, for the first time, how the blue-gray paint on the front porch is chipping. She wills herself into the scene, the sun hot on her face, the house dark and shadowed in the light so that it looks melancholy and out of place in the brightness. This time, she doesn't go past the house. She hoods her eyes and comes up the steps, opens the front door and steps into a parlor from another century.

She wanders the hallway, the airy rooms with their high ceilings and large windows. A thin layer of dust is on the furniture and the sun pierces through the white curtains and paints the floorboards gold. She comes into a room with a tall, four-poster bed. It is a peaceful room with curtains that billow inward only to be sucked out against the long and broad window frame. Lila climbs onto the worn bed and listens. For a long time, silence. Then Alma is reading to her. She hears, "This is the way of our dust—briefly illuminated, forming itself into clay and one long arc of desire. Slipping across a field as if it's forever."

"Who wrote that?" she asks.

"A patient of mine," Alma says.

"Go on," she whispers.

"And then you are the one whose body misfires. An inner comet trailing its cellular dust everywhere. And it is toxic only until you realize that we all come to that path, that bridge between this world and the next. And whether you had seen it coming or not, whether you are strong enough or not, you are strong enough."

Max

It is only one p.m. and I'm spent. Early release at Tyler's day care and he not wanting to leave and screaming and throwing his Cheerios all over the car. And I think—he must know. On some level, he must know. Nothing would comfort him. For two hours he screamed when we got home, until he fell asleep, exhausted, in his high chair and I don't even dare try and transfer him to his crib.

Sadie will be over in an hour to take care of him. She's taken the week off from work so she can be here at a moment's notice. When she arrives, I'll drive into the city, cross the Styx to that quiet room beyond which I can't follow Lila. I can't fathom it, that she will be gone.

I'm wandering the house trying not to think, but thinking again and again about last night, when I arrived at Lila's room. She had asked me to come back alone and Sadie had come to stay with Tyler. I walked into the room and Alma and Samantha were there on either side of the bed. Samantha was stroking Lila's hand and Alma was holding a notebook and reading to Lila and everything was otherwise silent. A nurse began to wheel in a tray, then retreated. And I thought, is this some sort of last rite? Does everyone but me know something here? And a panic began to crawl up from my belly. I heard something behind me and it was Darryl of all people. I saw him freeze in the doorway as he took in the scene. *Fool*, I wanted to say. *You are a fool*, but when I looked at him again I saw that it was registering, that he was starting to cry and I thought, well, maybe there is still something inside that mess of a man. I was watching all of this unfold and I thought, they are trying to help me hold this. They will not let me do this alone and I loved all of them suddenly and fiercely, a love like a substance, viscous and full.

✿ ✿ ✿

I tiptoe into the kitchen and Tyler is finally in that deep, passed-out state in which I can move him. I lift him carefully and carry him upstairs, lower him into the crib, turn on the monitor and close the door. I peer into Lila's office, the new guest room. No visitors last night. Darryl had come in alone and today, for the first time, the bed is made. And then the doorbell rings. I must have gotten the time wrong, I think, because it's still too early for Sadie to arrive. And I open the door and it's the Polish girl, Alenka. She smiles shyly. "Is okay? I left you a note that I come back on Friday."

No worries—I want to tell her—the house doesn't need it, but she is looking past me at Tyler's toys strewn all over the floor and from where we stand, we both see a tower of dishes in the sink. She smiles and walks past me, begins to gather Tyler's toys and put them in the large baskets. Then she heads to the kitchen. I find excuses to come in and out and finally I escape to the living room and sit down with the paper. I hear the water stop and silence. When I look up she is standing in front of me.

"Your wife," she says. "Sadie told me. I'm sorry."

I nod like an idiot when what I really want to say is, "Don't—please don't," because six months' worth of the crying I haven't let myself do is gathering in my throat. She sits down next to me. "My mother," she says. "My mother was sick."

"I'm sorry," I say, and I see her suddenly—a small blonde girl by the side of a bed like Lila's—and then I see Tyler when I brought him in the night before last and he was crying for Lila and she barely had the strength to hold him. Of course, I think, what could he understand?—and then it's there—all of it—and I cover my face in front of this woman I don't know and I'm sobbing. She sits there for a few minutes and then, before I can think, her arms are around me and my face is against the soft fabric of her shirt.

"Is okay," she whispers.

She is holding me the way one would hold a child and then she begins saying something in Polish. She goes on and on and I am listening. I have no idea what she's saying but whether she means to or not, she is changing the rules and then of their own volition, my lips make their way down the front of her shirt. She stiffens in surprise and I think to myself, "stop," and then I feel her hand stroke my cheek.

Is this what you want, pity sex? I hear myself think. And her hand in my hair is unsure. My mouth has found its way past her bra to her breast. It is already in my mouth and it is wondrous. A car starts nearby and we both stop for a moment. I realize we are in front of the large, bare windows, but she is ahead of me. She pulls me away from the couch and begins to lead me into what is now Darryl's bedroom, then reconsiders and leads us up two flights of stairs to the small room on the third floor.

She must have found it when she cleaned, my cave with its TV and books and awful shag rug. She turns from me so that I will not see her face. *Run,* I tell myself, but then she pulls her T-shirt over her head. She opens her jeans and steps out of them. She reaches and unhooks her bra and I come up behind her and slip my arms around her tiny waist. Six months of hunger: I am pressed against her, about to kiss her neck when suddenly, without any warning, it is there, filling me—a rush of love. For a moment, it attaches itself to the feel of her skin against my skin, to her tiny shoulder blade, to the soft dune of her hip; but it is ridiculous, this love that has hinged itself to lust, that has found me in this wrong place, followed me into this room. And then I lose it—all desire is gone—and there, still breathing beneath the press of my body, beneath its admission and then its shame, a woman I don't know, waiting.

I sit down on the floor, my head on my knees. There is no excuse for what almost happened except that I no longer believe I will survive Lila's death. Then I hear it, clear as anything, Lila's voice in my head. It is the same voice, hoarse and sweet and exhausted when, after thirty hours of labor, the nurse put Tyler in her arms. *Look at him,* Lila said. *Look at him.* Only this time she's saying, *I have to go, babe.* And I wrap myself around her voice, even if I am the ventriloquist who brought it into the room. *You can't leave,* I tell her. Alenka begins to get dressed. She turns around to look at me and I look at her and she has the decency not to say anything. Faintly, I hear the front door close. Then the silence of the house like a wind thick with sand, erasing me.

Alma

Alma walks into the room, lifts the next chart. She shakes her mind free and tries to focus on the paper in her hand. Forty-two-year-old woman. Five miscarriages. Yes, Alma has seen her here before, when the screen refused to blink a heartbeat back at them. Her technician is out for the day and rather than call for a backup, she pulls on her gloves, spreads gel on the woman's belly. The woman's face is turned from her, bracing. Alma clicks to secure the cursor, measures the longitudinal view, then the transverse. She hovers the cursor above the image, then clicks, moves it down six millimeters, clicks again. Repeats the steps one more time. She turns the monitor gently toward the woman. "Come see this," she says and there, blinking almost in unison, not one but two tiny flashes of light.

Silence. Then "Oh my god. Can I call my husband?"

"Of course," Alma says. The woman reaches for her bag and her cell phone slips out and falls into a few pieces on the floor.

"I've got it," Alma says, and she puts the phone back together and hands it to the woman, and busies herself at the sink. The woman is laughing and crying into the phone, and Alma is glad she has her back to her because she herself is crying and she looks down at her hands in the dim light and they are suddenly an old lady's hands, the veins grown prominent, the treacherous insurrection of age. When had this happened?

Piercing her through and through is the love between these strangers she is overhearing, their palpable, well-earned joy. They are so far from knowing what can happen, what is unimaginable at a moment like this—that one day, the child or children who had, from the second they'd appeared like a radar pulse on a screen, become your whole life, could be coming apart because you could no longer hold their world together. Why isn't she trying to stop Darryl? What if it were Samantha careening out of control?

Some of her friends tell her that they'd seen this coming. Yet she and Darryl had wrested from the grips of two decades more joy than most. Last night in Lila's hospital room, she could feel Darryl's eyes on her and she'd wanted to shake him, and she'd wanted him gone, and she'd wanted to just go and slip her arms around his neck and ease herself onto his body. She thinks about asking one of the other attendings to take her next appointment and walking down to the river and with the calm of a previous certainty, dialing his cell phone; she imagines it as if it were a choice, to call him and simply tell him she still loves him. She imagines everything else, however briefly, receding from them like a spent tide, the anger, the score keeping, the trove of resentments, the betrayals and heartbreaks. But then does she really need to call him to get his answer? He's given her his answer.

The woman is off the phone and lying still, her eyes riveted to the screen. Alma comes back to stand beside her and then the woman asks quietly, as if it is the most terrifying question in the world, "The heartbeats—are they strong?"

"They are very strong," she tells her.

Saturday

Thirty miles north and a mile east, bits of seashell, a claw almost fossil, a bed of mud, granite sparkling: the edge of a day.

Darryl slams into the sunlight like a buck.

Max wakes with a start to find himself adrift in a large bed. A room away, Tyler blinks his eyes open, watches the clowns dangling overhead among the motes of dust sailing the room.

In the house at the end of the quiet cul de sac, the day begins like any other. Upstairs, Samantha blasts her music, drowning out the sound of her own thoughts. She doesn't hear the footsteps she might otherwise recognize as her father's coming up the stairs, the sound of his hand knocking shyly on her mother's door.

Alma, opening the door to find Darryl, discovers she can barely breathe, the moment in front of her as fragile as blown glass.

Later, arriving one after another from across town, as if they'd been summoned, stepping into that quiet and terrible room, they find Lila turned around and flat on her belly as if the edge of the bed were the lip of a cliff. As if what was just in front of her had drawn her there, all dazzle and light.

Venus in the Afternoon

It began like this: Megan woke up and pulled me toward her in that proprietary, non-sexual way I saw stretching ahead of us for years and years, and into the unsuspecting canyon of her neck I whispered, "Megi, this isn't going to work." Last night she'd done it—gotten me drunk, gotten herself drunk and asked me to marry her. I'd asked for the night to consider it. Now that I'd given her my answer, she began pounding her fists on my back, then rose from the bed, pulled from her drawers some of the clothes I kept at her apartment, and began tossing them out the window so that by the time I looked out, some of my favorite things were being picked through on 14th Street. I grabbed a suit she hadn't gotten to yet and barricaded myself in the bathroom. Before I left, I stood over her where she sat in the worn armchair, head down, quietly crying. I wanted to tell her so many things—how fine she was, how incredibly fine. What an ass I was.

"Don't," she said, in that weird, prescient way that women have of anticipating the stupid things we might say or do, and in a daze, I closed the door and began walking to work.

The sky was blood red, as if the sun had decided to set instead of rise. As soon as I walked into the office, it was clear that the universe was about to stick it back to me, like some

Western, accelerated, kick-ass karma. The smell of burnt coffee was spreading through the suite of offices. The lights flickered as if they didn't dare come on and each office had been padlocked so that we couldn't get in. "What the hell . . ." Stephenson muttered right behind me.

Later we would understand that we were just a hiccup, an early imperceptible blip in what would become the implosion of the dot com bubble. But no one had a name for it yet. Just outside the door, I stood still, like a horse refusing to leave the gate. All around me, the rest of New York was striding against the wind with extraordinary purpose—hightailing it off each curb the millisecond before the light changed, very much knowing where they were going.

But a few hours and gin and tonics later, I was on great terms with the city which was whirling by outside the window of the bar and growing increasingly more beautiful with every minute. Reading the paper over the shoulder of the woman next to me, I saw that Saura's *Carmen* was playing at the Thalia in 20 minutes and ran to catch it for the three-thousandth time.

The film began with its percussive stomping. A row of dancers with their swirling skirts, their backs straight and motionless, just the sharp declaration of their heels, each trying to outdo the other as they auditioned for the role of Carmen. Paco de Lucía was making love to his guitar and the dancing was more provocative than any graphic sex. Then the aisle was briefly flooded with light, and I turned to see who was entering so late, and in the seconds before everything went dark again, I saw her standing there, tall and lithe, with the dark hair of a gypsy reaching half-way down her leather jacket as she lifted herself onto her toes to scan the theater for a good seat.

It didn't surprise me that she looked to me like Pilar. How many times had I gone to Saura films, especially this one, hoping to find Pilar. I turned around for another look, but she was gone.

Then I was sucked back into the film, envying Antonio Gades his sullenness, the daily building of sexual tension as they danced at each other harder and harder. I even envied him his heartbreak. Because Megan had been so sweet, so well-intended that she had unwittingly returned to me the desire for women like the one pouting on the screen, who drew me, like devil's fire, to the edge of some dark and glittering abyss.

But then there she was, coming up the aisle as the credits ran and I couldn't believe it, it was Pilar. She walked right past me. I was on my feet in seconds, and slipping in behind her, put my hands over her eyes, then turned her toward me, and just as she was opening her eyes, kissed her slowly, first on one cheek, then the other, then on her forehead, then, when she didn't pull away, deep in her mouth. "Coño!" she said, freeing herself and taking a step back to look at me.

Without another word, she led me out of the theater and into a tiny charcoal-colored Mazda she'd parked at a hydrant and that was miraculously still there. She was wearing a miniscule skirt that was barely a reference to a skirt. She pulled out of a tight spot in three expert maneuvers, one hand on the wheel, the other on my leg. Her eyes were peeled forward, and a smile played on her lips. I had a thousand questions but none that couldn't wait for the imperatives of the moment. The lights of the city danced and blurred as we sped downtown. Then on the corner of 23rd and 6th, she stopped and squeezed into a spot the size of a shopping cart, took my hand, and led me up some stairs and into a dark apartment, then into a room without turning on the light.

❁ ❁ ❁

When I first woke, I was staring into a ceiling draped in a thousand scarves. The room smelled faintly of jasmine, and there beside me, half draped in a pale sheet, the still uncompromised hips and breasts of the woman whom I was convinced I still loved.

For a moment I let myself imagine that we had never left Sevilla. That Pilar had never felt the first stirrings of restlessness or left me for the bullfighter on a motorcycle. But beating back the edges of my sleep were memories only a few hours old of Pilar weaving through a phalanx of yellow cabs, of her conspiratorial smile as she led me up the stairs, of lifting her onto this bed, her tiny skirt still hitched around her hips, an incredibly sexy black lace bra erasing all thought, all knowledge, the blah blah blah that would come later.

The light was beginning to pierce through the slatted wooden blinds. The walls were a deep Ottoman red and whatever furniture there was lay buried beneath things that had been shed with little plan or purpose. In the corner, a pile of discarded dance shoes climbed up a wall. I pulled on my pants and headed down the hall to where I'd spotted the kitchen the night before, but stopped short at the sight of a boy at the table. His face placed him at about twelve or thirteen, but his body was wiry and small. He was wearing a black turtleneck that was too tight for him and wire-rimmed glasses that seemed too big. Long dark hair fell in front of his eyes but didn't hide his scowl as he took me in. He turned back to the book he was reading, then looked up and scrutinized me again with obvious displeasure.

"So which type are you?" he said, squinting up at me, "Goat cheese and basil omelet? Belgian waffle? Straight black coffee, or," he looked me up and down disdainfully, "Wheaties?"

"What do you think?"

He stood up and began to circle me. He was small but forbidding.

"Standard toast and coffee," he said dismissively. "Unremarkable taste. Low risk."

Low risk? I wanted to say.

Pilar had come into the room and stood behind him now, wrapped in a short, sea green silk kimono, her hair cascading down her shoulders.

"Grant, this is Julian, Julian—Grant," she said.

Julian seemed about to say something, but then held back, arching his eyebrows at Pilar reproachfully.

"You can stay," she said to me, ignoring Julian's glare, "but I've got to grab my books and run."

"What's she studying?" I asked Julian as soon as she left the room.

He hesitated, then, in a barely audible voice, said, "Auric photography and energy healing."

"Auric photography?"

"Yes, photography in which you analyze people's auras." Julian was trying to keep his face neutral but a side of his mouth was beginning to twitch with the effort.

✿ ✿ ✿

Pilar was born in New York but her paternal ancestors hailed originally from Spain, and on her mother's side from the dusty plains of Egypt. By the time I had met her nine months into my year and a half of writing in Sevilla, she had already run with the bulls in Pamplona, and could tip her head back and down as many *sol y sombras* as the most macho of the men. All this and she could also, without any warning, shrug back her thick mane of hair, tie her shawl around her skirt, then slip her fingers into well-worn castanets and begin to play the emotions in the room like Carmen letting loose her fire.

Pilar harbored a terrible taste in men. She had a weakness for the ones who were most in love with themselves, the ones who rose to their feet and stomped back in response, wanting more than anything to win the dance of seduction in public, to the envy of all the other men. Night after night, I scoured the bars for her, because I had joined the ranks of the smitten, and would watch her fly, beautiful head first, right into the flames.

The most offensive of them—before the bullfighter—was Romero, also known around town as "el Rey." Pilar stood up in Noche Azul that night and curled her hands in a seductive *braceo*. She wore a long red skirt and a tight black top that offered her breasts to the beholders. Just below her waist she had tied a shawl of butter-colored silk covered in scarlet roses. Her long fingers curled above her head then down like the fluttering of doves.

Romero bided his time, but when the guitars veered sharply into *bulerías*, he stood up and declared himself in heelwork that moved so fast, the black of his pants blurred into a swirl of movement. *Pilar*, I wanted to whisper, *don't*. I'd been there long enough to know he was an asshole and a womanizer. Weeks later, walking home from the seafood market, I came across her sitting on the steps of the church in the Plaza Virgen de los Reyes. She had her face in her hands and she was crying. I sat down beside her without saying a word, offered her a rumpled napkin. For ten minutes, I just sat there passing her, one after another, the bar napkins that had accumulated in my pockets, then when those were depleted, I offered her one of my shirt-sleeves, then the other. She started laughing then crying again and soon I was kissing her either cheek, her wet chin, and for the first time the bottomless bliss of her mouth.

She moved in with me and stayed for six months. In retrospect I would realize it was probably some kind of convalescence, but for me, without question, it was love. And there were moments, in the diminishing light of early evening, when she would come and throw her arms around me, hold onto me like a new swimmer to the shore, that I could have sworn she loved me back.

❁ ❁ ❁

Pilar was almost an hour late to our dinner at Punjab's on East 6th. She arrived blushing, apologetic, and annoyingly beautiful—her eyes glistening like an Egyptian cat's.

"I'm so sorry," she said. "I was having a bodywork session and all this stuff started coming up—"

I got up and stopped her with a kiss. The other diners quieted and watched us.

"Come sit," I said.

She pulled herself away and sat down.

"So," she said, from a safe distance. "Tell me everything. What have you been up to since Spain?"

"Well, I searched for you for years, then finally found you in a theater in New York."

"Seriously."

"I was doing some writing for a while, then I started an MBA."

She looked at me incredulous, "an MBA?"

"Yeah. Well, I had published the book of stories that I'd been writing in Spain and was doing the penniless, exploited adjunct thing, but managing to squeak by. I was in the middle of my second book when my mother got sick. Six months in and out of the hospital and we find out that my father has married his paralegal and dropped my mother from his insurance plan. She stood to lose the house, so I went to work. Got a job in the high tech world, did my MBA at night."

"That's incredible."

"Not really."

"And the writing?"

"I don't know. I've tried not to think about it."

"And you?" I said before she could ask anything else.

"And me . . ." She sighed deeply, but offered nothing.

"True love?" I asked. She looked away. "Thought so once or twice but nope, didn't work out. Julian is all the love I need."

"That's a lot for Julian to carry, no?"

She squinted at me. "Maybe," she said but her hand under the table was on my leg, unequivocally changing the subject.

☼ ☼ ☼

What is it about knowing something is doomed that gives you the secret keys and maps to a body, that gives the conversations between bodies a heady, dangerous air? Our bodies knew how to speak to one another and so for the next few weeks, we entered a feverish, obsessive tunnel—but in the small hours of the night, unwanted thoughts nagged at me—that I was falling in love with her again but that something from her side was still missing, just as it had always been.

☼ ☼ ☼

One morning, two weeks into our new affair, I snuck out to buy the closest thing I could find to *palmeras*. When Pilar came into the kitchen, I led her to the small table beneath the window. I fried an egg the way she had once liked it, sawed bread into thick crusty pieces and brewed a strong tea with cardamom pods floating to the top.

I placed the food in front of her, bent and kissed her neck. She looked away.

"There's no way back," she said. "If we tried to enter it again, it wouldn't be that."

"Yes, but it could be something else equally wonderful."

Her smile was coy and non-committal.

She was in the shower and I was sipping a second cup of tea when Julian passed through for his glass of orange juice and one of the croissants Pilar always picked up for him at the French bakery on 77th and Columbus. I didn't know what Latin intellectuals looked like, but Julian was how I was beginning to picture them: long, straight dark hair, a look of tortured intensity, mouth pinched, chin sharp, bones rising like scaffolding beneath the skin.

"You seem pretty comfortable here," he needled me, putting his glass down on the counter.

I looked at him trying hard not to smile. "I've known your mom from before you were born."

Now I'd gotten his interest. His eyes widened and he lifted himself out of the slouch that gave him the air of despair and ravage that usually comes with middle age.

"Where did you meet her?"

"Sevilla, 1987. We lived together."

"How long?"

"Six wonderful months."

"And why did you leave her?"

"What assumptions. Who ever said I left her?"

Julian turned away and poured himself more juice. "Not bad," he said gesturing at the table, "but it won't do you much good. You're not going to last."

"Thanks buddy," I said, and he slouched out of the room as if he was heading for a sharp-tongued editorial meeting, rather than for the more banal indignities of sixth grade.

❀ ❀ ❀

When we were together in Sevilla, Pilar had taught flamenco and been good enough to have a list a mile long of local *mozas* trying to get into her classes. Here she worked as a shiatsu therapist in the East Village above a tiny, heavily draped, post-Hungarian coffee shop renamed "The Crisis Café."

Her inner circle, which I was getting to know as I spent more and more nights at her house, consisted of either recent New Agers, like herself, or artists like Magdalena—a performance artist whose typical work consisted of painting her entire body, face and hair white, then standing for hours in Times Square, Washington Square, or Columbus Circle, balancing an apple in her open hand as her pet snake, who bore a luggage tag with the name "Original Sin" wound itself around her thigh.

She was perpetually trying to talk Pilar into participating in one of her creations—the latest being a piece she'd entitled "Venus in the Afternoon."

"It would be Venus at Middle Age—," Magdalena said, as she tried one more time to pitch the idea. "Still beautiful, but bearing also the scars of love."

They were sitting and sipping some wine as I reheated the Pad Thai I'd picked up on my way over.

"She could have her progeny by her side, or our take on who her progeny could have been," Magdalena continued, thinking out loud. Julian was sitting at the table, pretending to do some homework but now he looked up.

"Do you mean Eros?" he asked. "And are you talking about Aphrodite and Greek mythology or the Roman reworking of Aphrodite into Venus?"

"No no—," Magdalena interrupted him. "I was thinking of Peter Pan. With her eternal beauty, Venus would have by her side an eternal youth."

But before she'd finished her sentence, Julian had put his hands over his ears and left the room.

✿ ✿ ✿

A few days later, Pilar threw a small party for a good friend who had just published a book called *Your Negativity, Yourself.* This group of Pilar's friends wore an assortment of body-clinging exercise apparel and some had the beatific expression one usually sees among trust fund devotees in ashrams. They were not exactly my crowd but Pilar had met me at the door with a long, promising kiss and I was feeling hopeful. After an hour of being cornered by an anorexic woman in tights who was earnestly trying to explain Reiki, I excused myself and went to the bathroom. When I came out, I passed the half-open door of Julian's room. All I could see was a small bed buried under a huge mound of coats and a bookshelf that climbed to the ceiling, piled with books several layers thick. Julian had gone to a friend's to avoid the party, and the temptation to explore what he had always kept bolted was overwhelming. I was about to push open the door when Pilar grabbed my arm.

"There you are," she said, pulling me back into the living room. Someone had put on Enja and she was rolling her eyes. She reached up to a high shelf and took down a CD whose cover was overrun with a camp of gypsies, their flamenco guitars slung jauntily around their necks. "Shall we?" she said. And that's how we took over. I was not a dancer but years of amateur drumming had honed my ability to play around with rhythm, and in Sevilla I had managed to master *palmas*. Everyone stopped what they were doing to watch Pilar twirling to my percussive clapping. As the music gathered to a crescendo, she lifted her skirt to expose the red rose that was curled around the black silk of her stocking.

After the third dance, she bowed, put back on some ane-
mic music, winked at one of her friends, then led me through a
door I'd never noticed off the laundry room. We were on some
narrow back stairwell and there she lifted the flounce of her
skirt to reveal that she was wearing nothing but stockings that
ended in lace halfway up her thighs.

"You need me," I whispered into her ear later that night.
But I knew that it was myself I was trying to convince.
Because there in the dark of the stairwell, the words had
finally formed for what I had felt, years before, in Sevilla, and
what I felt balancing her against the wall, the flounce of her
flamenco skirt resting on my shoulders—that I could have been
absolutely anyone.

✹ ✹ ✹

The next morning she suddenly announced that she would
be leaving for a four-day meditation retreat at a place called
"Kripalu."

"You're running away again," I said, suddenly paranoid.

"I'm not running away."

"You're running away. What scares you?"

✹ ✹ ✹

A drink with Liam didn't help. "Man, you're doing it again,"
he said.

"No, I'm not. This is different."

"What came over you with Megan? You just sprang it
on her?"

"No, she gave me an ultimatum the night before, marry her
or move out. And then I just knew. But Pilar is something else—
one of those women that happens to you once in a lifetime. And
well, it's a package deal. She's got this weird, interesting kid."

"Of course she has a kid. It's always something—a husband, a history, a wee little drinking problem. Now it's a kid. You keep going back to these women with an edge because you're not doing what you want to be doing. It's your job you needed to leave, not Megan. She was a woman worth attaching to. This one—this is a rescue fantasy."

"You're so fucking off base. First of all, I've barely thought about Megan since I left, which I think speaks volumes. Second, if you met Pilar, you'd know in an instant that she hardly needs rescuing. And anyway," I continued, "who are you to give me advice?"

Liam was on his third wife. A serial marrier. When teased as to whether there was a pattern there, he said, sure there was a pattern—that his wives had all grown bitter and boring.

"I don't know man. If it's not a rescue fantasy, it's no less narcissistic. You probably want to be the one to tame her."

"Shut up," I said.

The first two days after Pilar left for her retreat, I moped and paced the small circumference of my neglected apartment. Every so often, I would remove from my pocket the incomparable note she'd left on my pillow. Pilar had always had abominable handwriting that seemed to dispense with critical letters every few words, so that where I'm sure she had meant to write "Let's speak," the note read, "Let's peak when I get back."

❁ ❁ ❁

With Pilar gone, I spent my days avoiding looking for a new job by hiding out in the back rooms of bookstores. I was at the Strand, buried in a worn hardcover copy of *Woman in the Dunes*, when I got the call from Concord Preparatory, Julian's school, saying that he'd suffered a bad fall while climbing the ropes in gym class and that Pilar had left them my number. I floored it uptown and found him slumped in a chair in the principal's office, his face an unnatural shade of white.

"Thanks," he mumbled without looking at me, as I helped him into the front seat of my car.

Five hours and an MRI later, I held Julian's arm as we climbed the stairs to my apartment. Where another day he might have sneered at my furniture, at my sparse décor, he barely gave it a glance. Instead he asked for the bathroom and before he could shut the door, was bent over, throwing up.

I heard the water running, then he stumbled out, paler than before. "Get into bed," I said, leading him to my room. "The doctor said it would be all right to sleep as long as I wake you every few hours." I pulled out the cot I kept in the closet and fell asleep next to him.

It must have been five in the morning when I opened my eyes to find Julian gone. I bolted up and then I saw him, climbing my bookshelf, reaching for something on the topmost shelf.

"Get the hell down," I said. "You shouldn't be doing that."

"What is this?" he asked, holding the book I had taken great care to conceal, especially from my own sight.

"A collection I wrote a long time ago," I said.

"And published with a good press," he added.

"Yes. Before I decided to study business. Give that to me."

I stood up and he handed the book to me shyly.

"Can we go back to my house?"

"Sure, but I don't have a key."

"I do," he said. He scooted down the bookshelf, then sat down on the floor like a three-year-old to put on his shoes.

✿ ✿ ✿

Once we'd let ourselves into the apartment, Julian avoided his room and went instead to Pilar's where fully clothed, he crawled under the covers.

"Wasn't Claire supposed to be staying with you?" I asked, looking around.

"Yeah, but the first day, she got a call that her mom had fallen, broken a hip or something. Anyway she left."

"And you didn't tell Pilar?"

Julian looked away. "She was really looking forward to this."

"Well, I can stay if you like," I said.

"Right," he said, sounding relieved.

Julian didn't seem to know what to say next and we both fixed our gaze on the books haphazardly piled on Pilar's night table. On top, the *I Ching*, and then the *Tibetan Book of the Dead*, but from there it deteriorated. *Know Your Aura*, *Kabbalah for Dummies* and a book cryptically called *The Cure*.

I glimpsed a photo album on the bottom shelf of her night table and reached for it. Julian looked embarrassed and once I started flipping through the pages, I could see why. It was a catalogue of Pilar's boyfriends—Pilar with this man, Pilar with that man.

"Which one is your dad?" I asked him.

Now Julian's face blossomed into a full blush. "Well she used to say, 'the universe,'" he said, smiling at me conspiratorially, "but finally one day she broke down and told me it was someone named Carlos Figuero."

"The bullfighter?" I asked.

"So she said."

Maybe, I thought to myself, and maybe not. After her affair with the bullfighter and my departure for New York, Pilar had no doubt had a wild stretch of consolation sex. She probably couldn't tell Julian who his true father was because she probably didn't know.

Julian began to twirl a finger through his hair, then looked me in the eye. "She says that she doesn't have the emotional room for you."

"I see. And who does she say this to?"

"Magdalena, Natasha, Claire, everybody."

"Well I don't give up easily," I said, and Julian avoided my eyes as if out of kindness.

✿ ✿ ✿

For twenty-four hours, we inhabited the apartment silently, as if we'd always known how to live side by side. We read on adjoining couches, ate our dinner while watching Herzog's *Fitzcarraldo*. On the evening that Pilar was due back, I was heading to the kitchen to prepare dinner when I saw that the door to his room was open just enough to render it a change in the state of affairs, maybe even an invitation. He was lying across his bed, a pad of paper in front of him.

I pushed the door open a little more and there, floor to ceiling, were books, hardcovers mainly, on a feverish scaffolding of shelves that filled every inch of space, pausing only briefly to accommodate an antique-looking dresser, the small bed. I looked around, whistling my appreciation. He had, in well-preserved hardcovers, a good deal of Rilke, the full collection of Nietzsche, every Russian novel under the sun.

"Pain or pleasure?" I asked him, pointing to the notebook open in front of him.

"Homework. Definitely pain."

"Can I help?"

Julian looked up surprised, as if no one had ever asked him this before, then shrugged. I looked over his shoulder at the title of his essay. "Schopenhauer's Lunchbox?"

"Yeah—Hendrick, my Humanities teacher, wants me to 'stay within the bounds,' as she loves to say. Anyway, she said that I could read whatever I want as long as my essays stay at a level the idiots in my class understand, which obviously means I can't write about any of the ideas of the philosophers or critics I'm really interested in. So she's left me no choice but to write about their lunchboxes—What each philosopher or literary critic might have in their lunchbox and why."

"What have you got so far?"

"Well Derrida was a challenge, but—well—tell me what you think." He picked up his pad of paper and began to read. "If we dared to open Derrida's lunchbox, we would probably find a web of faint but possible traces of food, none of which are truly present as such but rather depend on being woven with other traces in an endless, indeterminate coupling. So that Derrida's lunch is never completely present, never a thing unto itself, but is rather a swarm of quantum-like elements assembling and disassembling."

I laughed. "I would argue with you but I can't say I've ever understood a thing he's written."

Julian tried to suppress a smile but he was clearly pleased. "In Descartes's case," he continued, "his attitude toward his lunch illustrates his famous 'cogito.' He opens his lunchbox but doubts that his lunch is real. After hours of doubt, and still hungry, he is rewarded by the realization that there is at least one thing that is definite, and that is that this entity that is thinking and doubting must exist. The cogito is, of course, challenged by many thinkers on many fronts and so Descartes forgets about his lunch—which in any case he can't establish is truly there, and his health begins to deteriorate."

Julian threw down the pad and it landed with a thunk on the bed.

"But I'm nowhere at all with Kant or Heidegger."

"Let me help you. What do I read?

"You could start with these," Julian said, piling a thick stack of books into my arms.

¤ ¤ ¤

I began to read small snippets of Kant, whole chapters of Heidegger. I had fallen asleep in the middle of a particularly obtuse chapter of *Being and Time* when I heard the heavy thud of Pilar's bags as she dropped them on the floor and closed the door.

¤ ¤ ¤

Pilar came back positively glowing, and at first I thought maybe there really was something to these retreats. But when for the fourth time at breakfast she mentioned the Shiatsu master from Boston, Julian and I both knew the terrible truth.

Pilar stopped sleeping with me, though she still seemed content to have me in her bed, so that each day I awoke a knot of misery and desire.

A few days later, Pilar brought the Shiatsu master home for dinner. He was in town only briefly, he said. He couldn't stay. He looked me in the eye inquisitively as if trying to figure out my role in this ersatz household. Whatever his name had been he had renamed himself Orion. Or Ori, as Pilar called him.

Ori had the aging Jewish face of someone whose tribal affiliation was insisting itself onto his universalist identity. Julian and I knew immediately where this was headed. Ori never missed a mirror or a look of studied bliss when the conversation grew too loud for him and he retreated to some other plane, watching us like a god. After dinner, Pilar left to walk Ori to his train and returned hours later, her hair disheveled, her lipstick smudged past her mouth.

"You don't know who you are," I yelled at her that night, not accustomed to my own voice filled with rage. "Thirteen fucking years later and you still want to be the one desired by the biggest preening bastard. What's it going to take?"

※ ※ ※

A few days later, I gave up and listlessly began to throw my things into the overnight bag that was still tucked under her bed. My timing was awful. Julian was just walking in from school. He surprised both of us by throwing his arms around me. Before heading to the door, I stopped and looked back at him, his skinny body, his old old eyes. Who were we? There was no name for our bond; it existed only by virtue of this woman who, for all intents and purposes, was leaving me for the second time in two decades.

"Don't go back to computers. You can really write," he said.

"You think so?"

"I do," he said, handing me back my book that he'd apparently filched.

"And I expect that you'll review me one day."

"I will. And I will skewer you."

"I look forward to it," I said, and turned away quickly before he could see my face.

※ ※ ※

What is it about heartbreak that allows you to see so clearly? It was all spread out before me suddenly, the whole sordid human drama. Men, women throwing themselves at the first hint of love like gamblers betting their entire hand.

When I left Pilar's house, I spent my days alternately swearing off of love, or sitting in cafés perusing the endless crowds, as if the city would lift her again like a wave, and deposit her, ideally with Julian, right at my feet. That's when I began to see them—the characters that would come to inhabit my new stories—in the cafés or walking up the avenue, not knowing that I was about to tip them into an adventure that would unravel their harsh urban armor, leave them new again and exposed. I threw myself into a whole slew of new stories and they came toward me like lovers, mysterious, confessional, lusty, or fragile.

When Stephenson called a month later to lure me into the startup he'd joined, I was torn, but I made a promise to myself, and I kept it, waking every day at five to write for several hours before heading off to work. Then, my mind still rumbling with way too much coffee and the aftershocks of an image or scene, I would make my way to where it would be waiting for me—as constant as the sun itself—my new fluorescent-lit cubicle.

Today, though, I was grateful for the soothing whir of the servers, for the predictable, somnambulant mood in the front reception. Yesterday my boss had thrown me a difficult development glitch that had the tech gurus in knots and that no one else wanted to touch. It was clear that a great deal hinged on my finding a solution, the reputation on which I'd just been hired, and perhaps most importantly, my ability to keep up and support my new writing life.

When I finally stepped outside, the afternoon shimmered in the storefronts. The sun was a seething orange-pink disk about to impale itself on the needle of the Chrysler Building. Instead of taking the subway home, I decided to walk all the way down to the Village and see if I could rustle up Liam and a couple more friends to come out and celebrate. Because, after hours and hours of wrestling, I had done it, clinched the final algorithm that had stumped us for weeks.

The sun had dropped. I was just crossing Washington Square Park when I spotted a small crowd. I drew closer and there, perched on a platform draped with gold cloth, wearing a gold lamé bikini, with every inch of her sprayed gold to the tips of her eyelashes, was Magdalena, her eyes peeled forward, her breath low and barely audible. She lifted her arms slowly and when both arms were at shoulder height, a gust of brilliant lorikeets suddenly lifted from the cages that were at her feet and lined themselves up and down her arms and in the crook of her neck, their wings flapping, as if they were going to return her to the sun. Then, in a bluster of color, they took off, circled overhead, then reassembled on her arms. She stood perfectly still, without even blinking as the crowd applauded. She remained like that for five minutes, the only movement, the rustling of the birds. Then, in a barely perceptible movement, her left arm slowly pointed downward and the parakeets flew in an unchoreographed wave into the two huge cages that waited open on the ground.

Once the crowd had dispersed, I came up to her.

"Not bad," I said. "Might be one of your best!"

"It's you—how are you?" She stepped back to look at me.

"I'm good. How about you?"

"I'm fine." She hesitated, then looked up at me, her green eyes sparkling, "but Pilar's a wreck."

"Oh?"

Magdalena sighed. "Well first the Shiatsu master turned out to be married."

"What a surprise."

"And then Carlos—Carlos came to New York."

"The bullfighter?"

"Yeah. His marriage fell apart and he looked her up and found her. He arrived just like that with bushels of flowers and a few pieces of gaudy family jewelry and right at her front door told her he had never stopped loving her. Then he saw Julian and totally freaked. Thinks he's his, though Pilar won't confirm it. Anyway he's extended his ticket and he's insisting on paternity testing."

Magdalena was throwing shiny gold covers over the bird cages which she zipped closed.

"And Julian?"

"Moping as usual. Of course he's been keeping you front and center, and I can tell you that you're the first."

"Listen," she said, picking up the heap of gold robes she had shrugged off behind her. "I'm about to meet up with Pilar in Times Square." She was about to say something else, but I didn't wait around to hear what it was.

"I'll meet you there," I said, before she could continue and took off for the subway as she began to gather her things.

⚬ ⚬ ⚬

The train stopped and started, crept forward and creaked, and I tried not to think about what I was doing. When I ran up the stairs at the corner of 46th and 7th, I was plunged into a large, motley crowd that seemed to be trying all at once to move forward, everyone craning their necks to see something just ahead of them. I pushed my way deep into the mass of bodies until I could see what they were all staring at. There in a huge polished conch shell stood Pilar, bare but for some gauzy sheeting draped over her breasts and wrapped around her body just below the waist, and then trailing down to the ground where it transformed into the glistening green tulle at her feet.

This Venus was tattooed. She had the names of all of the men who had loved her inked onto her body in such a way that made it look as if they were to blame for any corrosion of her beauty; some of the names were dark, some fading, and others very pale, as if they had been etched long ago. I scanned for my name. Had I been given a breast? A golden thigh? The intimacy of her belly? Was I engraved, like wisdom itself, right between her large almond eyes?

No, there I was, faint and fading, and as far as possible from her heart, circling her ankle like a bruise. But instead of the old familiar pain, it simply provoked a smile, and right then I knew that finally I was no longer in love with her.

Next to her, hanging by an almost invisible wire that had been strung from the top of the lamppost, in what must have been the ultimate concession in the name of loyalty and love, was Julian as Peter Pan.

Venus's eyes were closed, her mouth opened slightly, as if in the first adagio of sex. Without opening her eyes, she threw her hair back over her shoulder as she used to do when she danced, and gracefully shifted her weight, then grew still again.

Maybe it was something about her position. Her eyes closed, her face at once longing and sated—which made her, of course, such a perfect Venus—desire and pleasure alternating in sure-fire milliseconds. Maybe it was the lift of her hip, or the way one leg bent elegantly over the other. Maybe it was the diaphanous fabric that brought back to me the gauzy bed sheets of our flat in Sevilla, but it came to me all at once—a memory that had gone unvisited, that had been lost in the alcoholic haze in which it had occurred, but that came back to me all of a sudden, whole and clear.

The night she had tiptoed in at four in the morning to find me waiting up in bed, with six empty beer bottles on the night table beside me. She had confessed then that she was seeing the bullfighter and broken me into a million pieces. "We are done," she had said, and she too had started to cry. I lay on my back, my hands covering my face and she came to sit beside me. "I'm sorry, my love," she said, and the "my love" that slid so easily from her tongue seemed suddenly like the trite whispers of a prostitute. This was what I was thinking as she started to stroke me the way a mother would to comfort a child, but it was not comfort that she provoked, and to save me from the shame of it, she climbed on top of me for the last time that decade—her hair brushing my chest. Then, she kissed my cheek and went out the door.

I looked at Julian. He hung motionless as if this was something he had always done. Without his glasses, I knew that the crowd must be a dizzy blur of faces and perhaps this allowed him the illusion that his features were no clearer to anyone else. His legs looked terribly thin in their green tights, the feather in his felt hat ruffled in the wind. His hair lifted in the breeze, his eyes barely blinked. How had I never noticed the hint of a dimple in his cheek, the way his nose arched and lifted?

Other than that, his face had no trace of me; there he was all Pilar, but how many times had I stared at his hands not knowing why they stopped me, at the thin, awkward angles of his body, not understanding why they seemed so familiar, why they provoked in me such bittersweet feelings.

I hadn't seen it, in the way that the mind doesn't see what it's not looking for.

A murmur was gathering and swelling around me and I turned to see the gold sweep of Magdalena's robes—the ones I knew that she would likely remove with great ceremony— parting the growing crowd. But before she could reach Pilar and Julian, I pushed my way up front. I stashed my paper under one arm, tightened my trench coat and held my briefcase with a Monday morning's determination as I took my place, the perfectly invisible commuter, right beside Venus and Peter Pan, like the alternative from which they flew.

A wonderful thing, I thought, performance art.

I trained my eyes forward and commanded them not to blink, but just before I did, I saw Julian's eyes widen and the edges of his mouth fight back a smile as he caught sight of me. Pilar was still oblivious and I secured my gaze on the Times Square ticker with the wild hope that if I stared long enough, it would begin to spell out for me in brilliant and flowing letters how the rest of this story would go.

Waltz on East 6th Street

I

Years ago, Aunt Renata squeezed a picture into my hand when my mother wasn't looking. Aunt Renata wasn't really my aunt, but rather someone to whom my mother had clung like a sister, like blood.

In the picture, my mother is thin but she is wearing a pale belted dress with a flared skirt and she is smiling. That is, her mouth is smiling. Her eyes are unreadable, her cheeks taut. There is a tree just behind her and the smallest hint of a fence. I have studied the picture a thousand times trying to figure out whether this was in one of the camps. The dress belies that possibility but still the fence looks menacing, cage-like and my mother's expression is strained and odd. On the back of the picture, in German, and in a masculine script, it says only "Spring." Aunt Renata said she had found the picture when they were liberated from the camp. She won't tell me anything else.

❀ ❀ ❀

My mother was a beautiful woman. Even now it's obvious—her bearing still regal, her cheekbones high and proud. She never talks about her experiences and her silence walks the house like the ghosts that accompany her. She was 17 and had snuck out in search of food when the Gestapo came to collect her family. She was caught a few days later and shipped from Prague to the first of several camps. That's all I know, and I don't even think she was the one to tell me.

There is so much I have wanted to ask her but she's never offered up anything but silence. The next part of her story is a void, a portal between dimensions that I dare not enter. Her words, when she speaks, are carefully chosen. I watch her move around the house like a spy in her own life, surprised to have found herself capable of holding a baby, of pulling weeds, her skin glowing, alive.

✧ ✧ ✧

Throughout my childhood I waited for death to claim her. As if I didn't dare believe her stay of execution, surprised again and again to find her moving about the kitchen in the morning, preparing her strong coffee then settling into her favorite chair by the window, not a figment of my imagination, not a dream I had dreamt.

In school, when I would perform in the annual play, I would peer out from between the curtains to make sure she was really there. But there she would be, sitting quietly in one of the front rows amid the chatty American-born mothers with whom she had nothing in common, the long sleeves of her simple but elegant dress hiding the number on her arm. I would see her looking around, as if she were once again wondering whether she had done the right thing by putting me in this Jewish school with its fortress-like walls, its windowless brick.

Alongside her would be a sprinkling of fathers who had rushed home early from work or rearranged their schedules to join their wives at the plays. I knew little about my own father except that my mother had met him in one of the DP camps, then lost track of him. A decade later they remet and were briefly married but he'd died when I was just a baby, ultimately succumbing to the ravage that had been done to his organs in Birkenau. Growing up, I couldn't imagine what it might be like to have a father. My mother and I were plant and soil. We were a greenhouse, hermetically sealed. But lately, she seems to me paler, thinner. As if the reserve she had all those years, the strength with which she raised me and urged me far from the dark banks of her memories—as if that were finally dwindling.

Last week, when I entered her apartment unannounced, I caught her staring, unblinking, out the front window as if it held a view other than of a New York City street, as if her memories, rather than receding, were coming finally to greet her. It took all I had at that moment to hold back from asking her, *When will you tell me?*

II

It was a few days after that visit that some of my own memories came flooding in to haunt me. On my way home from work, I had slipped into my favorite bookstore with the idea of treating myself to a new novel. But once in the store, I found myself stopping instead in front of a dark wooden bookcase entitled World War II where a book I'd avoided about the children of survivors stared out at me. I pulled the thin book off the shelf, took a deep breath, and opened it in the middle.

I don't know how long I stood there reading. I just remember at various junctures wanting to stop, but not being able to. It was as if someone had found all of the secrets of my childhood. All the quirks and odd behaviors, the ghosts and the inhabited silence. I was reading a section describing the different paths that survivors had taken with regard to their religious beliefs, either complete renunciation or complete acceptance, with a few sustaining a complicated and ambivalent relationship with both. I thought about the Jewish school my mother had put me in, but then otherwise seemed to want to avoid, and then about her relief when I asked to leave it and disappeared, indistinguishable from the others, into a vast public school. She never censored me or criticized as I transferred from school to school, from persona to persona. As if she thought—of course—how could it be otherwise?

What she did for me was hold the course. Grab onto her life and steady it as much as she could, let me know that at any moment, I had a place to land, and if necessary, to hide.

I looked up for a moment to check the time on the old brass clock that hung high above the bookshelves. And that's when I saw him. Older, his face thinner and lightly lined but lit by the same shock of wavy blond hair. There was no question that it was he. His name was Jürgen and on that strange and disturbing night on which we had met twenty years earlier, he had just arrived to New York from Berlin. That night, I had learned little else about him. I was about to stop him and say hello when he continued past me down the non-fiction aisle, then turned out of sight.

He doesn't know me, I thought. *He doesn't remember.* And it all came back to me, as if all those years hadn't passed, as if just the night before I'd rested my head on his shoulder, felt his arm around my waist, his cheek a breath from mine.

He didn't know into what he had wandered that Saturday night, in the East Village, any more than my friends and I knew yet who we really were, what we were hiding. He had just flown in to begin his graduate degree in philosophy at Yale and someone had brought him, oblivious to what would take place. A party was a party. We were young, and we thought, very chic. Globe hoppers. Citizens of the world. We flirted with the edge. Offered ourselves to whatever abyss we could conjure. None of us had figured out yet that all of our parents had survived the camps. We'd simply met our last year at NYU and congealed like a tribe of abandoned children. We didn't know and didn't yet wonder what we were looking for in all the clubs and parties we sought at that time, in the excesses of alcohol and whatever fashionable drug lined the bathroom sink like a ritual offering.

This particular party was hosted by Zuna something, I can't remember her last name, only that her parents were presumably diplomats living in London, and that she had piled her hair high on her head and secured it there with little cocktail forks. Someone in our group had met her at an art opening and had brought us along like extended family.

The party was in Zuna's East Village apartment in which walls had been broken down to create a loft. Here and there a private space was carved out by a piece of dark cloth, or by curtains made of long strips of eight-millimeter film.

We arrived like the refugees we were into this dark room. Like speakers of an underground language, we had learned to find our way to the drugs that inevitably were served up at these evenings. One by one we went into the bathroom where a friend of Zuna's was offering opium from tiny bits of foil.

When I came out, someone had turned off the raucous punk music and put on a waltz. As a joke I'm sure, but suddenly the large and shadowed loft, with its brooding ceiling murals, seemed like a large chandeliered hall. Some couples stood up laughing and struck poses of affected elegance. It was quite a sight—at least 80 people, most in different shades of black, some ears sporting skeletons, crossbones, some heads shaved, all dancing as if at a grand ball in Vienna.

I was watching Varda—the only other woman in our group—dance with Isaac, her glittering scarf, her long black dress, her dark hair flying like a gypsy's after her. It was then that I felt Jürgen's hand on my arm. Tall and blond, with a sweet smile, he didn't say anything, just led me to the floor, wrapped his arm around my waist and began initiating me into the trance of the waltz. He was a superb dancer and if I didn't think about what my legs were doing, it felt effortless.

The room began to spin. One two three. One two three. He pulled me closer until we were flying as one body. It took a while before I looked up from that whirling, hypnotic dance and realized that my friends had all stopped dancing. From different corners of the room, they stood watching us, voyeurs to their own deepest horror and desire. And I understood from their expressions that the sight of us was somehow both thrilling and disturbing. The *Ubermensch* extending his arm to the Jewess. I knew then that I held all of their expectations, unarticulated, unimagined, all of their hopes that I would continue to rise to the occasion, that I would dance at least as gracefully as he, that somehow I might even introduce some new element, redeeming, transcendent. And I was thinking this when all of a sudden Jürgen somehow missed a beat and, still following the rhythm, I tripped over his foot and fell on my side.

"I'm so sorry. Are you okay?" Jürgen crouched down beside me. But as he did, I could suddenly feel the rage in the room and had I been able to, I would have pushed Jürgen away as Isaac rushed toward us, pulled him to his feet and away from me, then punched him in the face. Then, within seconds, as if some signal had been sent out, the rest of our group moved in on him. Before Jürgen could recover, his stunned hand just beginning to move to his cheek, they surrounded him and lifted him into the air, Rafa and Nano grabbing his legs, Isaac and Uri supporting the weight of his shoulders and back.

"Bastard," they hissed as they carried him toward one of the loft's large windows. "Son of a bitch."

"What are you doing?" he yelled, as they held down his struggling arms, grabbed someone's scarf off the coat hook and tied it around his kicking feet. They hoisted him head first out the window, holding him by his bound feet and dangling him over the pavement six floors below.

And Jürgen hung over East 6th Street like a sacrifice. Like everything that had never been said. Like the demons unmentioned, alongside which we had all been raised. In the closets that were sealed and stuck, the long dim hallways of the apartment buildings that collected every nation's misery, the hallways in which we'd grown up. Even when we had moved to the suburbs, our cars full, our windows down, shadows followed us. Trap doors. Hatches. There were more lamps in my house than in any house I have ever known. Lights were left burning. Flowers planted in every inch of soil.

☼ ☼ ☼

Some people on the edge of the crowd saw what was happening and stopped dancing. Zuna and I started yelling at Isaac and at the others. We rushed to the window, leaned out on either side of Jürgen, offering him our arms. He grabbed my arm with one hand then Zuna's and we pulled him as hard as we could toward us.

"Untie his legs," I yelled at Nano as we pulled him fully inside. Jürgen brushed himself off and left quickly, slamming the door. The moment was over. If there was shame, no one rose to claim it. Someone quickly changed the music. Isaac, Uri, Rafa and Nano retreated to a corner. When the crowd had thinned out, the rest of us collapsed exhausted in various corners of the large room. Zuna threw blankets over us and I remember wondering, before I fell asleep, why we had never realized it, why we had never talked about what it was that joined us. I remembered the thick darkness of Isaac's mother's house when we'd all visited once, Nano's father who worked three jobs and who never met our eyes, about whom I was later to hear the whispered accusation, "Kapo."

✿ ✿ ✿

The next morning, I went to see my mother. There were no words to describe what had happened, not the events themselves, but rather that I had known then, in a new way, what was at the core of my being, what I needed to grapple with.

My mother didn't hear me come in. She was cutting vegetables on the large marble counter in her kitchen, listening to her favorite classical music station. Mozart's *Piano Concerto No. 27* concluded and then the radio show host introduced the famous Strauss waltz—*Voices of Spring*. As the music began to play, my mother froze where she stood and the color drained from her face. She stared blankly at a corner of the room until I coughed and she looked up. Slowly her eyes began to register the present moment and her arms, trembling slightly, opened wide to greet me. She held me tightly to her, then released me.

"Coffee?" she asked.

"Sure."

She reached for two of her best ceramic mugs. Ground some beans. This was how it had always been. The small rituals that held us. But I could no longer keep my part of the bargain.

Her back was to me as she poured boiling water into the French press. The knotted bun that held her hair was almost all white now. A brilliant white pierced by a red lacquered hair stick.

"Mom, what happened?"

She turned to look at me, holding the carafe. "What do you mean?"

"During the war, what happened?"

For a second her eyes held mine, then she turned from me. The carafe shook in her hands, the coffee sloshing up the sides. She set it down. When she turned back to look at me, she was livid.

"Why are you doing this?"

"I'm not—I just—are you ever going to tell me?"

She turned, giving me her back and just stood there.

"There's nothing to tell," she said, and left the room.

III

How much time is left?

Is it fair of me to want to know what she lived through?

I am beginning to lose faith that she will be able to tell me. Still I wait. I tiptoe around the fortress of her silence, waiting to glimpse even the slightest easing. She obviously knows now what I need. But ultimately, the choice is hers. Only she can be the gatekeeper of her memory.

Meanwhile, I have begun to construct tales. I hang them next to one another like the panels of a triptych, try them in this, then that array. I move them, shift them, look at them in the light of different days. When I've come close, I tell myself, when I've captured some of the true essence of her story, I will know.

In one of these stories, which hangs alone, without a frame, without beginning or end, my mother is being waltzed around a small room. The man she is dancing with has removed his jacket and draped it over a chair, its insignias and swastika for the moment unseen. He clutches the waist of the pale dress he has her put on for these occasions.

One two three. One two three. She follows the man's step carefully, trying not to think beyond this dance. Instead, she tries to imagine that beneath her hand is not a stiff brown fabric, but instead a jacket of linen and silk. That Strauss's *Voices of Spring* is not locked inside this small room, but is reaching up into the cathedral ceiling of a vast and brilliantly lit hall. That beyond this room is not barbed wire but the glistening streets of a city. One two three, one two three. Her body continues to obey the rhythm but she suddenly knows what it is that will redeem her. For a moment her cheek goes soft, her eyes blaze with light as she reaches several decades forward to touch me, as she dreams me into being.

Flammable Vacations

To understand how and why I left the sanity of my husband to go on vacation with my mother, you would have to understand that nothing else could have ended my ambivalence and helped me make the decision I needed to make, and that I was sure that a few days with my mother would. You would also need to understand the absolute sanctity for my mother of things that were on sale, or worse, things that were free, so that when she won a weekend in the country in a sweepstakes, I knew it would be easier to agree to go than to withstand her unrelenting pressure.

Early on in our relationship my husband would say, "Stand up to her." He was new then to me and to her. Now, years later, he understood. When my mother made up her mind about something, you had the choice of taking her on vertically and being hit head on, or lying down and letting her wheels just graze you. Those were the choices.

※ ※ ※

I didn't see my mother often. But I received bits of her weekly, sometimes daily. Not letters or postcards but odd items that arrived like their own Morse code. Items for which she had accumulated coupons or found in one more sale she couldn't resist. It didn't matter how irrelevant, she would send away for anything that was free and have it shipped to my doorstep, mutant and unwanted, then to my sister's doorstep across the country and to anyone else in the family she could equip.

Only my husband was never a recipient. As if to say, if you were truly one of us, look at what could be yours. And he looked, at the adult diapers ("Save them," she had said, "you never know."), at the issues of discontinued bridal magazines (we had eloped), amused and relieved that he was not on her distribution list. Lately there had been a profusion of little boys' underwear. *Irregular*, they were marked across the crotch.

"What if I turn out to be infertile?" I asked when the third such package arrived. "What will it be like to have all these piles of underwear waiting to be filled? And why all boys?"

"You're right," she answered. "We should leave God his free choice. I will start buying some of those pink vitamins I saw on sale at the drug store."

"I thought we were the ones who are supposed to have free choice," I said.

"Good point," she responded, her voice tight and clipped lest I dare interrupt. "So admit that you've married that man just to spite me and choose again."

✿ ✿ ✿

About twice a year I would brace myself and visit her in New York. I always flew down. I knew that if my mother respected little else, she respected the strict arrival and departure of planes and I was therefore almost always guaranteed a clean exit. For a day or two before flying down, I would grow quiet, confusion gathering around me like so much baggage. Dante would sense it and circle me tentatively, knowing that I experienced these visits as perilous but necessary, that they pulled me away from him like some silent undertow, then crashed me back up against him bruised and only occasionally wiser.

It was on my most recent trip to see my mother that I had gotten caught in the net of this vacation. We were eating lunch—or rather I was eating lunch and my mother was pacing, cleaning a spot here, a corner there. This act was somewhat comical to me because all that was really visible of any surface were the small areas that weren't covered by newspapers, clippings and books. She was always flushed and excited to see me, as if something in her was stirred up by my arrival. Perhaps to channel this excitement, she prepared elaborate meals on the days that I visited, which she served immediately, regardless of the hour. Today it was Hungarian goulash which I was trying to get down at eleven a.m. She had taken out a setting of good holiday china and placed it delicately in the clearing she had made with her elbows between two teetering piles of papers and books.

While I ate, she stabbed with her cloth at a corner of the table. We were having a conversation we'd had many times before.

"You look tired," she said.

"I am tired."

"Why don't you take a short vacation?"

"I can't do that right now. My business is really starting to grow."

"Helen, tutoring is not a business. And it is certainly not a career. Not after all the school we put you through."

"Mother. Don't start."

"Of course I have no doubt that you need the extra income. Marrying a musician, really! I mean all the money we poured into your education before your father died and what have you done?"

"I'm asking you not to start."

"Did we not compliment you enough? You are so beautiful. So brilliant. Why are you pouring yourself down the drain? What caused you to have such low self-esteem? Tell me because I really want to understand it. Was it that I didn't work all those years? That you didn't see me using my mind?"

You've used your mind up, I thought.

"You know Jonathan Zimmerman is still single. I ran into his mother at the supermarket. He's doing cosmetic surgery—it's true that it's not all that brainy—I would prefer someone working on a cure for cancer, but I'm sure some of the time he must use his skills to heal some people badly smashed up in an accident or burn victims, perhaps. Do you remember Mrs. Rosenthal on the corner? Well—"

"Enough. You spend six months telling me that I don't come to see you and when I do you've prepared an elaborate torture chamber."

"You are funny. Why don't you go and work as a comedian? Then the two of you can perform on the street. And a street musician! Really! How do you know where he's been?" She paused. "At least the Philharmonic!"

"Okay. Enough. There are things that you can't trample on. Off limits. The subject of my husband is off limits. So can we just stop? I'm not used to this anymore. My brain cells have gotten used to linear thoughts, linear conversations. It took a long time but it happened."

"And what kind of conversations do you have with that man? I'll bet he doesn't even read."

"He reads what interests him."

"And what's that?"

I mentally scanned his night stand. *Musician, Keyboard, Jazz*, some catalogs from high-tech music software companies.

"What interests him."

She was silent for a long moment.

"And what kind of parents name their child Inferno?"

"It's Dante, Mother. Not Inferno."

✿ ✿ ✿

Just give up, I told myself. *There is no way of reaching her. Just do what you've always done. Sit very still.* I waited five seconds. Ten seconds. She wasn't saying anything. How many hours till my flight? Three, four, oh god, how was I going to do it? I saw her coming closer to me with her cloth.

I wasn't tasting my food. Just swallowing it to avoid the questions about why I wasn't eating. When I looked up, she was almost upon me, about to lift my plate and clean the table under it. "Mother, I am not done eating," I said with as much control as I could muster. "And I'm not done being married."

She put the cloth down, smiled and began to open the mail piled on the other end of the table. That's when she found it—the announcement that she had won a weekend in a cabin in Vermont. For herself and up to three guests.

"Oh look at this," she said, waving the letter in the air. "I've won a vacation. You'll come with me, of course."

"I don't think so."

"Don't tell me that nonsense again about your work. I'm sure you can move around a lesson or two. You know I haven't had a vacation since your father died."

There it was. I lifted the letter.

"A cabin in Vermont in December?"

"We'll keep the heat up."

"Mother I don't think there'll be heat. Do you even know how to make a fire?"

"Oh no, I don't like fires. Didn't I ever tell you what happened to the house on Chauncey Street?"

I knew the story inside out. How my aunt Sylvie had been playing with matches, how the house had gone up in seconds, how they'd just made it out. How Aunt Sylvie had been clutching her ragged yellow bunny when the fireman grabbed her and passed her out through the window.

❉ ❉ ❉

Of course I could have said no. But the truth was that there was something compelling me. Lately, I'd found myself contemplating motherhood, and ever since this idea had begun to consume me, I was feeling more and more distant from Dante, peering at him with a disturbing new lens. With every day that passed, I found myself wondering: Was this the man I wanted to father my child? Was this the man I wanted to be bound to forever? I had enough friends who had already traversed that territory to know that once you had a child, no matter how the marriage turned out, you had that child's other parent forever.

Just a few nights ago, I was on the brink of falling asleep when I heard Dante come in with a couple of guys from his band. I could hear beer cans snapping open, the silence and the one-line firings of non-verbal men. There was nothing wrong with any of that, nothing new, but suddenly I'd imagined a small boy in the doorway rubbing his eyes open, looking for his father. I had harbored—and I should say that this was my fantasy and never Dante's—the hope that one day Dante would be discovered, invited to play on the great stages. It was not because I craved any of the material rewards that might accompany that, but because I truly believed in his talent and was still clinging to the notion that such talent would find its proper recognition. But suddenly for the first time I asked myself: *What if it didn't?* And I imagined that little boy a few years older on an outing with his friends, passing his father, gray hair receding, playing his latest composition on that same street and I thought, *god no, that won't work.*

Quickly I caught myself. *That's mother talking.*

No it's not. It's me.

☼ ☼ ☼

The next day on my way to work, I stopped by a dark window that gave me back to myself cold and wrapped in a faux fur that had seen better days. My mother was right. I did look tired. The city was already in its first tinsel for the upcoming holidays. I turned the corner and found myself in front of the city's most glittering department store, its windows sparkling, none of the cheap stuff, no tacky holiday dressing here, but real stars and slivers of moon, bits of the galaxy. One was invited in to be part of a cosmic event, to transform.

I followed, as if called, right into the cosmetics galaxy, and up to the counter of my favorite Italian master. The salesgirls were dark olive-eyed creatures with lips the color of sunburst, with breasts that rose unaided like a Madonna's, eyes that forgave me but still seemed wary of the disorganization of my face, my clothes.

There was a young woman ahead of me. From what I could overhear, she was trying on different looks for her upcoming wedding. The man who was dabbing at her face stepped back as if he were perfecting a masterpiece.

"With your pale skin and dark hair, your look is very European," he said approvingly. "Very Chanel."

What would he say to me? I wondered. Your look is exhausted Hungarian, the collapse of Eastern Europe. We can fix it.

He wasn't even glancing over to where I had perched myself on a stool behind the woman he was fussing over. He didn't look as if he had any intention of relinquishing her face that begged one more hint here, shadow there. Should I give this up? Fate did not seem to be on my side and usually I knew not to push it. But I didn't move. Just sat there like a Russian housewife waiting for bread.

☼ ☼ ☼

"Ah yes," he said when he finally got to me. "Ah yes." He circled me like a problem, a dilemma he was not thrilled to have encountered. At some point I heard him whisper, "Clarity, clarity. We need some clarity."

"Exactly," I said.

"The question," he said stepping back, "is which way do you want to go?"

To my own surprise, my eyes filled with tears. "That's what I don't know."

"All right. All right. For today, I can decide, but at some point, you will have to make a commitment."

When he finished, I looked in the mirror. My cheeks held a hint of blush, my eyes were aglitter in a dusky blue, my lips a 1940s red. There I was, sultry as a movie star, a woman who could do it all and still look ravishing. I looked up at him beseechingly. "Should I do it? Should I have a child with my husband?"

He was silent for a moment.

"Is there someone else you want to have a child with?"

"No."

"Well then," he clucked, "it doesn't all have to be that complicated, does it?"

I walked home slowly, catching myself in every glass, in the eyes of men who for the first time in months let their glance hang those extra few seconds that made it no longer a glance but a question, an invitation.

I had a new face. I could be anyone at that moment. Start again. Tabula rasa. Fall in love perhaps with one of these men in tweeds from England or in a Burberry coat. I could wander down to the medical area if I really wanted to make my mother happy, put my newly glamorized self right in the lair of doctors.

Why Dante?

I didn't know why Dante. I couldn't explain him any more than I could understand how I ever decided anything. I had always simply let my heart rule. When I'd met Dante, I had fallen immediately, unequivocally in love. With his voice, with the beauty of his lyrics, the days that never knew where they would go. The parties, the gatherings that would spring from nothing, people from every country filling our small rooms. With his boundless generosity and kindness. When my mother's voice would rear itself inside my head in those days—*But how will you live? What kind of life will you have?*—it was easy enough to turn down the volume. He would become, I would say, who he was supposed to be. But this desire to have a child—to swell up with this little person, to know it, to love it—had caught me suddenly in its imperatives and erased any certainty.

Dante was clear about wanting a baby and was excited. He thought that we were ready, that it was time. But every day, I equivocated. Was my mother right when she said that I had married him to spite her, that I had mistakenly thought that by marrying so far from who she was I could finally cut that throbbing cord that still hung between us?

"Let me do it for you," she had said the day I told her we had married, stabbing at the air with imaginary scissors. "You don't need to destroy your life at every step to tell me you are an adult." She had begun snipping maniacally in the air. "There. You're free. There. Go."

✿ ✿ ✿

Hours later, the makeup scrubbed off my face, my body curled around Dante, I took a deep breath and said, "I'm going up to Vermont next weekend with my mother."

Dante moved back. Scanned my face in the dark.

"What's up?"

"What do you mean, what's up?"

"Going to Vermont with your mother? You're leaving me."

"No," I said quietly and took a deep breath. "I just need to go."

"You don't need to go. You don't need to keep doing this."

"Keep doing what?"

"This thing that you do," he said hesitantly, "I don't know, it just never seems to—" I heard a quick intake of breath, as if he were going to say something more, then silence. I rolled onto my side, watched the tiny silver and bronze encased mirrors I had hung on the wall sparkle with the passage of random headlights. I waited for a long while until I knew that Dante had given up on my responding and had fallen asleep. I turned over and moved closer to him, draped a leg over his leg, buried my face in his neck. I stayed awake for a long time, twisting my fingers round and round in his long black hair so that I could not so easily disentangle.

✿ ✿ ✿

I met my mother at South Station. To my horror, she emerged from the train with three bulging shopping bags in each hand, her large strong hands strained and chapped with the load they carried.

"What do you have in there?"

"Oh just some food, a few books, some things I thought we would need."

She set the bags down on the platform and began looking around. She had not been up to Boston since Dante and I had eloped. She had never once visited our apartment. Now she peered at the train station and at the people weaving around us as if they might reveal some clues about who I was, about why I'd made the choices I'd made. I noticed that under her coat, she was wearing a dress and nylons with her ever-present sensible shoes. I hoped that somewhere amongst her things she had brought some warm clothes.

We dragged the bags out to the car.

"Why did you park so far?" she asked panting, though by now I had taken the heavier bags off her hands.

"This was the best I could do," I said.

We pulled out and headed up 93 North. She looked awkward and uncomfortable, gazing out the window, her legs primly tucked to the side.

"Well—I came with you," I said.

"Yes, you did."

"And maybe," she continued, "it will help you get a bit of rest. Get rid of those dark circles under your eyes. I certainly didn't have to work as hard as you do at your age."

"Please don't start," I said. "I'm here to keep you company."

"Well, it's very thoughtful of you to have come but you needn't have done it because you think I'm lonely. I'm not." She paused, then drew in her breath and said, "Anyway, Sylvie is joining us."

"She is?" I was stunned. I loved my aunt Sylvie, but the news had caught me completely by surprise.

"How will she get there?"

"We're going to pick her up at the bus station in White River Junction."

"Well, thanks for letting me know." I felt close to tears though I didn't know why. *Why the hell had I come?*

"You can't be alone with me, can you?" I blurted out before I even knew what I was going to say.

"What do you mean? What nonsense!"

"No, it's not nonsense. You don't know how to be alone with me. What are you afraid of?"

"I don't know what you're talking about. Is this more of your therapy mumbo jumbo? Those people all need their heads screwed on straight. Maybe you could find some better things to do with your money."

I glared at the road for the rest of the way and she leaned as far as she could toward the door, the landscape whizzing by on her right.

✿ ✿ ✿

It was already dark when we met Aunt Sylvie at the bus station. She beamed when she spotted us. She looked even stranger than when I'd last seen her. She was wearing shiny black and white saddle shoes and her ruddy cheeks flushed when she saw us—like a twelve-year-old about to embark on an outing. The only problem was that she was sixty-five. Her mind was slipping backwards and as it did, she was reclaiming all of her lost joy. The wife and mother whom everyone had wanted to escape had simply stepped out of the life she'd been living and begun to retrace her steps.

It had started when I was in college. She'd begun to compose collages out of magazine pictures—baboons, balloons, whatever caught her fancy. She would send them to me with no explanation. Postcards from a mind gleeful, retreating.

What a pair she and my mother made greeting one another.

There was not an era that they belonged to. They were their own era, their own territory.

"Helen!" Sylvie rushed up and embraced me, then turned to my mother.

"Doesn't she look wonderful!"

My mother's brow furrowed but she remained silent.

✿ ✿ ✿

We found the small cluster of cabins down some narrow ice-covered roads that made no concessions for my car's width, its smooth city tires. The proprietor, alerted no doubt by the skidding of my car, was waiting for us as we pulled in.

"Estelle Goldberg," my mother announced rolling down the window. "I believe we have a reservation." The proprietor looked from my mother to me to the half-lit face of my aunt behind me. Judging by his expression, he had never before seen people arrive in dressy city coats.

"Are you women going to be okay?" he asked, half-concerned, half-amused.

"We'll be fine," my mother said in a tone that permitted no more questions.

"Well, pull your car in right over there," he said, indicating a relatively level patch of mud. "We walk from here."

A line of dark wood cabins formed an arc off to our left. Unassuming, they hung back from the lake, their roofs brushed and shadowed by the trees that grew thickly just behind them. On the right side of the lake, more trees as far as the eye could see, lifting on a gradual incline away from the water.

The proprietor led us down a trail of mud and ice. I saw him glance at Sylvie's saddle shoes which were becoming streaked with mud. At the furthermost cabin, with the heel of his boot, he kicked opened the door. He pulled out a lighter, lit the lantern he was carrying, and placed it on a small wooden table that shook for a few moments from side to side. My mother scowled. She immediately removed the lantern and put it on a shelf that looked a bit more stable.

"Do you ladies need some help getting the fire going?" He gestured over to the substantial woodpile.

"Oh no—"

Before my mother could say anything, I turned to the man and said, "Thanks. We're all set."

He shrugged and left.

I opened my bag, began handing out what in a flash of foresight I had thought to bring: thick camping socks, wool scarves, gloves. My mother and Sylvie accepted them silently.

Then Sylvie turned to me. "You know just the other day, I had a dream that you were expecting a baby."

"Well," I stammered, "I—we—I am thinking about it."

"You are?" my mother whipped around to look at me. "Why haven't you told me?"

"Because I haven't told myself yet whether or not I want to do it."

"Well one thing I know," my mother said, "is that when there's something you want to do, you jump in, even if you know it will end badly. You've always done it. As if you want to see if you can land in one piece."

"How wonderful," Sylvie exclaimed.

My mother brushed from her face a loose strand of gray-streaked chestnut hair.

"Well I would have preferred different circumstances—but I'm not getting any younger."

"Isn't it just wonderful!" Sylvie exclaimed again. "Can you remind me of the name of your husband?"

"Dante."

"Yes, Dante." Everyone was quiet for a moment.

"Well," mother said, "he has a good chin."

"Well, that's just great," I said and headed angrily for the door. "Thank you for that contribution!"

But my mother's attention was on Sylvie who had unzipped her bag to reveal that she'd brought no clothing whatsoever, just a stash of board games. They were entranced, unpacking the boxes like nine-year-olds.

I left them and went outside, walked down to the water and just stood there for a few minutes. The lake was like the flip side of the strange mood I had escaped. Dark, silent, inviting.

I approached but hung back from the lake's edge, as if it could have curled a dark arm around my leg and pulled me into its depth. I thought I'd take a walk to clear my head, and began to trace the edge of the water. I had been walking for about ten minutes when I turned around to find some landmarks lest I lose sight of the cabin. But in the cattails that grew between the cabin and the lake, I saw flames, billowing in the night wind. I ran back as fast as I could to find Sylvie standing in front of a fire, some matches in her hand, watching the flames with hypnotic fascination. I peeled off the thick shawl I had wrapped around my coat and threw it on top of the burning brush. Sylvie had a strange look on her face. Gently, I eased the matches from between her fingers.

My mother emerged from the cabin striding purposefully toward us. The expression on her face said that she'd seen none of it.

"What's going on?"

"I don't know but somehow this fire got set," I said.

"Such a fine girl, your Helen," Sylvie said.

✿ ✿ ✿

"Mom," I said, pulling her aside. "She needs help. Do you understand? If I had seen it just a moment later, the fire would have gotten completely out of control."

"Well it didn't did it?"

"Well that's because I—"

"Don't worry about her," she said, interrupting me. "She's fine."

"She's not fine."

"She's fine. Don't be so childish. Not everyone has to shove their skeletons out of the closet. You put your best foot forward in life. You don't need to make public every little personality quirk in your family."

"Personality quirk? Mother, for god's sake."

"Don't talk to me like that. And anyway, you help yourself. Don't worry so much about everyone else. Sylvie," she called out to my aunt, who still stood by the burnt stalks, "let's go inside."

✿ ✿ ✿

I walked away. *Okay*, I thought, *you wanted a push, so here it is. Go ahead.* I reached for the card of birth control pills that I had slipped into my pocket and walked up to the edge of the water.

I popped one out and tossed it far across the water. I threw another and then another. I looked back toward the cabin. Were they watching me? I put the rest back into my pocket, veered a bit into the trees and began walking, keeping my eyes on the water. The moon was high and almost full. The branches bent and brushed one another with their bare and twisted limbs. The ground crunched beneath my feet. Dead leaves, twigs, frost. I started walking faster. *Where are you going to escape to now?* I heard my mother saying. *Always escaping. Even as a child you built elaborate castles, then when they were close to completion, you kicked them to dust.* I walked faster and faster. The forest was growing darker as I moved away from the moonlit water. I took out the small flashlight I had stuck in my pocket and held it in front of me, illuminating the thick trunks of trees.

When I had gone deep enough into the woods that I was sure they wouldn't be able to see me, I leaned against a tree and crouched down. The wind was lifting and lowering the branches, scattering the fallen leaves and setting them down again. Here and there, I heard some scurrying movements, thought I saw the darting shadow of a small animal rushing back into hiding. Then a rustle just to the left of me and a raccoon dashed out from behind a tree. Right behind it, a cub emerged tentatively, trying to follow its mother, who turned and hissed until it reluctantly turned around and went back to their den. I watched the mother sniff the ground, lift something in her teeth and head back in the direction from which she'd come.

I couldn't move, though I was beginning to feel very cold. Some tears were blurring my vision. An old sadness rising. So that was it, was it? So simple, so banal, this wanting so viscerally, so simply, a mother. The old quest. The old pain. Had I hoped that somehow in this harsh and brittle place, some natural softness might emerge, some instinct to draw near me, to protect me, some hint so that I might know whether I could do this simple, incomprehensible thing of becoming a mother? That in this unlikely place, she might finally shed her crocodile skin and talk to me like a mother to a daughter? But as always, it was not to be.

I don't know how long I sat there. I was cold but the tears kept coming. Then finally they stopped. I heard a lone bird call out and another respond from what seemed like some distance.

I missed Dante. I conjured his lovely face, his long body. I knew that if he were with me right now, he'd be sitting silently by my side, watching the secret movement of the forest, listening to the soft brush of the branches as they lifted and lowered in the night wind. I remembered our trip to Mexico right after we eloped. We'd hunted for and found a strip of beach not yet overtaken by tourists. When we arrived, Dante had walked along the water's edge as I sat with our unpacked camping gear and watched him. The sun was setting over the beach and the sand was a color between copper and gold. He had brought only a few small instruments with him and at that moment he sat down by the water and began to play a flute. The music lifted and flew in all directions as the sky erupted into formations of purple and gold just above the water. And suddenly, there in the woods, as clearly as I had ever known anything, I knew that Dante was not the problem. That child looking at his father would see a man who knew his own passion.

"Okay," I whispered, "All right."

I took my birth control pills out of my pocket, popped the remaining pills one by one into my hand, and began to scatter them as I wove between the trees, the forest suddenly beautiful and fecund.

I could hear the lake lapping softly against the rocks and began walking in the direction of the sound. I reached the shoreline and headed in the direction of the cabins. I could see two lights in the distance around the bend. The light on the far left, I knew, was the proprietor's cabin. The one on the far right could only be ours. But something didn't seem right. The light was not the soft yellow of the lantern we'd been given, but a strange burnt orange. *Not again.* My heart started pounding and I began to run. When I reached the cabin, I threw the door open. My mother and Sylvie looked up, startled, from their chairs, my mother reading the *New York Times Book Review* and Sylvie knitting what looked like a tiny sleeve. Their feet were propped up on crates in front of the glow of a long and large propane heater.

"Where did this come from?" I asked, incredulous.

Sylvie looked up at me quizzically.

"What do you mean, dear?" she said. "It was in the trunk of your car under the blankets with a note saying to make sure we vented the room." She glanced over her shoulder at the window to her left which had been propped open with a book. "Your mother had never used one of these before, but I showed her how I thought one should light it."

I stared at her face. For a second I thought she had winked.

"Dante," I said, laughing. "It must have been Dante."

"Well, he certainly takes good care of you," Sylvie said smiling, and went back to her knitting.

My mother did not look up from her reading but I could detect an unfamiliar air of contentment in the small movement of her stockinged feet even as she shook her head disapprovingly at something she was reading, licked a finger and turned the page.

Fault Lines

The door to the orphanage is large and red, like a gash in the thick, gray stone wall. On a Sunday, four times a year, one of the nuns firmly takes her hand and walks her to the front door to greet her mother. These visits, she knows, are not for her. Even at six she knows this. The door always opens like a portal to another world and her mother is suddenly standing there, frightening in her beauty, red hair blossoming in long, manic curls, only occasionally held in check by the random grasp of a jeweled hairpin, tears that come immediately and easily which she dabs with a lace handkerchief, her face turned to the side.

Then her mother bends down in her long sleek dress, or in her slender wool coat with its cuffs of ermine until her eyes meet Michaela's. Her mother's eyes always ask terrible questions—terrible because they beg not for truth but for the lie that will allow her to once again leave, that will tell her—yes, I am all right. I don't need you. Go.

She doesn't need a calendar to know the advent of her mother's visit. The nuns grow tender, their hands brushing her hair more gently and with twice the strokes. Small treasures of gold-wrapped chocolate begin to appear under her pillow. Bits of conversation swim toward her at night when they think she's asleep.

"Three breakdowns," she hears them whisper.

"This poor child left and left again every time."

"Three breakdowns, can you imagine?"

Her mother's hands are the palest white. Not cruel. Fragile even. Bracelets rippling up her arms like water. A thin diamond watch ticking silently its own secret time.

She imagines her mother as a light porcelain doll cracking like an eggshell—small seams along her face, a long fissure down her spine, her flaming hair floating down in filaments.

On the days when her mother visits, the nuns wheel a tray of food to where they are seated in the garden that slopes gracefully down to the banks of the Hudson. Homemade pastries and an antique silver teapot that her mother caresses gently with her long hands.

Her mother never touches her. She wants so much to sit in her mother's lap but she doesn't dare ask. Instead she sips the honey-frothed milk the nuns have poured for her and answers her mother's questions about her teachers.

☼ ☼ ☼

On her seventh birthday, her mother enters carrying a fancy cake, her eyes sparkling with the adventure. Everyone stops and stares at the ballerinas performing pirouettes, at the prima ballerina on the thin icy peak, twirling gracefully on her toe without ever losing her balance. But this time, as her mother stands up to leave, Michaela reaches out and clings to her pale crepe skirt. She throws herself onto the ground, holding tightly onto her mother's skirt and kicks the ground until her shoes are caked with mud. "Take me home," she yells.

"Don't do this," her mother begs.

She looks up to see if her mother is shattering into a thousand tiny pieces. Instead she sees her green eyes afloat in tears. Her mother bends her head, makes the sign of the cross and begins to pray.

"I don't want to see you anymore," Michaela says. Her face is by her mother's shoes which are the color of pearl.

"Don't come back," she screams and runs before any of them can grab her.

Twelve weeks come and go, a season passes. She tiptoes to the door though no one leads her. No one takes her by the hand, though she knows that it's the day. She peers up at Sister Francis and Sister Alice.

"Where is she?" she asks. She can hear the panic in her own voice.

"I didn't mean it. Was it because of what I said?" Could they please tell her mother that she didn't mean it. She just needed to reappear. She could leave again whenever she liked. But her mother doesn't return.

Sister Francis's skirt. The warm folds of curtain by the vestry. Her bed in the dormitory with its scent of spring flowers. All of these become home. The corner in Sister Francis's office where she curls up by the radiator with her books. The chapel with its velvet and hush. The catechism like a melody. The confessional like a time machine that allows her to stay in the present, to exchange the prickling of her sins for the sweet sleep of forgiveness.

Home. The boarding school apparently paid for by her invisible mother. The girls are from all over the world so she is not the only one detached from family.

When Sister Francis visits, all of the sadness she's held at bay comes toward her like a tidal wave. Sister Francis holds her, rubs her back, kneads muscles that are permanently knotted.

They walk all around the grounds. Sister Francis's silence is like a beautiful lake. Michaela feels like a blade of grass beside the lake. The wind plays with her hair. Leaves rustle, then are still, their veins full of secrets.

⚬ ⚬ ⚬

Home. 116th Street and Riverside Drive, the white silence of her own apartment in the days before she begins Columbia.

Sister Francis helps her move in. Even in New York City, this invites some glances, the tiny nun in her crisp habit lifting boxes, heaving suitcases out of the back of her car.

When it's time to part, Michaela hugs her fiercely.

"Did she ever write to you?" she summons the nerve to ask. "Write to me?"

Sister Francis is silent.

"Can I have her address?" she whispers.

"Let it go, dear heart," Sister Francis replies.

⚬ ⚬ ⚬

At first Michaela loves her new life, the overflowing banquet of knowledge. She begins to write poetry, devours Rimbaud and Verlaine.

She is drawn to the broken ones. She can spot them in any crowd, sadness etched into the lines of their faces. She begins to date a young man in one of her classes. He doesn't tell her much, but she knows that there is a story by the way he needs to be constantly moving. He initiates her into the sweet oblivion of drugs, the hidden map of her own body.

One fall day, she's following a trail in Morningside Park when she sees a woman in the distance ahead of her, walking a tiny dog. The woman's frame is long and narrow and her long curls, which reach just past her shoulders, are the color of sunset. Michaela begins to run. She approaches the woman, taps her quickly on the shoulder before she can regret it. The woman who turns around looks at her blankly. She is much too young to be her mother.

But things don't go back to where they were. The fault line of her grief has been cracked open, and just a few months into her second year, she bolts.

✿ ✿ ✿

Home becomes the feel of her leather traveling bag—the one she uses as a pillow on a beach in Marbella, sits on in the Egyptian desert, props under her head on European trains. Her hungers are insatiable. She has begun to chase beauty, harshness, the edge of every experience.

She is traveling with no clear destination. At night she takes refuge in an exhausted sleep, or in the heat of greedy, angry sex. Every night, her sleep is swollen, bloated with faces of people she barely knows.

When she arrives to the inky shoreline of Crete, it welcomes her like a prodigal child. There are other of the world's orphans clinging to the beaches, easing from day into night as if that itself were a worthy occupation. At sunset, she wanders among their beckoning fires, partakes of wine, hash, skin offered shyly or brazenly. Everyone is running, though they barely move. She knows it in the way their eyes never search out her story. She knows it in the urgency with which they

clutch at one another, in the fisherman's coves, and sometimes in full view on the night sand. Sometimes she can't
bear it—the moments when her life begins and ends again in
someone's arms, the moments of tenderness going nowhere.
Sometimes she wants to snap the neck she's kissing, wants the
body crushing her against a wall of rock to crush her harder
until she crumbles, dust to dust. Sometimes it takes everything
she has not to say—Erase me—Now.

Then one night, the light is fading and she is sitting with
a German couple she's met and sultry Lydia from Barcelona
as they silently build a cage of sticks for their night fire. She
squints into the haze at a figure coming slowly toward them
from far up the beach, and for a moment, she thinks it's her
childhood image of Jesus, his hair blowing back off his shoulders, the wind whipping a loose garment around his body.

"Who is that?" Lydia asks.

"It's Johann," the German woman proclaims.

He joins them and sits down across from her. His face is
the kindest face she has ever seen. Lydia pulls out some wine,
passes it around.

From the conversation swirling around her, she learns that
Johann is a builder and that soon he will return to Amsterdam.
For a brief moment he meets Michaela's eyes and she lowers
her gaze. When the others say good night and drag their sleeping bags up the beach, the two of them sit silently watching the
fire as it dies out.

"Are those your things?" he asks finally, pointing to her
leather bag.

She nods and he lifts it and takes her hand.

He leads her a long way up the beach until a dark crest of
rocks juts out into the sea and they can go no further. He clam-
bers up and then reaches down to help her. She follows him

carefully as they climb around the bend to a stretch of beach she has never seen. In the beam of his flashlight she sees a tent-like structure of pale cloth, held up by long pieces of wood and weighted to the sand by large slabs of rock.

As they come up to the tent, she takes the flashlight from him and shines it to reveal colorful rugs covering the floor, pillows and cushions faded from use.

That night she's almost shy—the grace of his body, how little she remembers about being gentle.

Johann's arms feel like a continent. His nomadic house feels like it will last forever.

On the third night, she starts to tell him everything, from the beginning, and the way he looks at her, the way he gathers her into his arms lets loose such a flood of sadness that she doesn't know how to stop it.

✿ ✿ ✿

She follows him to Amsterdam and suddenly she is able to see it, the sun spilling off the rooftops like burnished honey, the canals glistening, the currents always moving. The streets thrum with rhythm. She doesn't run now but walks, taking it all in. One day she catches sight of herself in the dark glass of a shop. For a moment, she doesn't recognize the image that looks directly back, a face aglow, a body loved.

✿ ✿ ✿

They have settled into a rooftop apartment in the Jordaan. Three days a week she teaches English at a girls' school nearby. On the other days, as soon as Johann leaves for work, she drapes his old shirts around her and paints the small sloping rooms colors she has gathered from the city. The tiny kitchen, a burnt gold, its shutters, the thick cream of Dutch milk. For

Johann's workroom she chooses the deep hazel of the water, for their bedroom, the lavender of dusk.

So this is what it is, home.

She fills window boxes with bulbs of geraniums and tulips. She understands now why people persevere. How they rise and greet the day, glad to just be.

When her classes draw to an end, a hive of nine-year-old girls surrounds her. She watches with longing as their mothers arrive to collect them. The girls don't even glance at the door—so sure are they that when the time comes, their mothers will appear. There are moments when she wants to trade places and be allowed to leave with one of the mothers. But then she'll come home and the sun will be setting behind the rooftops, casting a beautiful light into her new rooms. She'll settle into a large old chair and read until she hears Johann's step on the stairs.

Johann is always building. He builds cabinets for the golden kitchen, a box of many layers for her jewelry. One day he builds her a birdhouse with four separate feeders and hangs it on the rooftop. She lies on the old, threadbare rug that they have placed on a flat patch of roof, watching the birds swoop down in clusters, eat quickly and nervously, then dart away.

"Stay," she whispers. "It's safe here."

✿ ✿ ✿

At the beginning of spring, her period is late. The day that she finally buys it—the little plastic test—takes it into the bathroom of a café and then waits, time slows, then stops. She doesn't know what she's hoping for. When the little line appears from nowhere she is terrified. A one-way arrow. She can't imagine how one does it—loves one's child day and night.

But Johann knows only joy at the idea of having a baby. He brings home the finest wood he can buy. Merbau and Dark Red Meranti from the forests of Malaysia. A cradle begins to take shape. Like a tiny ark, it sits in their room. And she understands the image. She understands that this baby and Johann and these little rooms are her transport to a world remade.

She sends Sister Francis pictures. Johann standing behind her in the kitchen, his arms swaddling her large belly. The two of them picnicking on the rug on the roof. Them, beaming at the camera, on a bridge over the swollen Amstel.

"You are almost," she writes to Sister Francis, "a grandmother," and laughs at her own daring.

✿ ✿ ✿

Then one day, afternoon stretches into evening and Johann is not yet home. Johann's boss is at the door when she opens it. A man of about sixty with four sons of his own, Gregor begins to cry before he can speak.

"New equipment," she hears. "Snapped. Instantly. I'm so sorry."

He stays for a while and then for a few more hours, afraid to leave her. She is crying so desperately, her big belly heaving as if it were going to empty itself right then and there. He is getting ready to leave when she suddenly stops crying and looks down at the pool of fluid by her feet. He calls for an ambulance but as the crew rushes in the door, it's too late to move her to the hospital. One of the men gets down on his knees next to where she lies on the rug. *Pers*, he says gently to her in Dutch.

But she turns away.

"You can do it," he whispers. "*Pers*. Push."

She lies defiantly still.

Gregor comes close to her face. He brushes a strand of hair from her eyes, takes one of her hands in his. This man who hasn't left her, this man who clearly loved Johann. He takes her hand like a father.

She closes her eyes and pushes with all her strength. Then again with the next contraction, and again. One of the medics hands Gregor gloves. In one long exhale, she feels the baby slide out. Gregor lifts the baby and holds him up to where she can see him, and they all stare in silence at the beautiful baby boy with hair the color of fire, and eyes, when he finally blinks them open, the color of the sea.

✲ ✲ ✲

Dear Michaela,

In the dark, it wasn't clear how much the baby looked like her mother. The small lines at the side of his mouth, the bright hair like a wheat field seared in the sun.

My blossom that I dropped.

Loosened from her breast, Sebastian's mouth was still puckered, his face soft. Though he was asleep, his lips still made sucking motions, searching the empty air for her breast. Outside, the discordant sounds of New York rushed by, snatches of music, the wail of sirens. Still the baby slept.

I am so so sorry.

For the first few weeks in Amsterdam without Johann, she'd kept going with sheer will and adrenaline. Finding a babysitter, teaching her classes, going everywhere with Sebastian strapped to her chest. But every evening in the terrible silence of their house, Michaela would find herself waiting breathlessly, as if this time, she would really hear it, the key turning in the downstairs door, Johann's long legs taking the steps two or three at a time.

It had been too much to bear, the sudden emptiness. Too cruel, the love she remembered in those rooms. And so she had sold all of their things and arrived in New York with just a single bag and Sebastian.

How could I have known?

As soon as she'd found the apartment and bought a second-hand car, she had strapped Sebastian into a car seat and headed upstate. The light danced on the road in front of her, patterned by the fronds of trees. For a moment, she was almost hopeful. If the universe could yield a day like this. If the sun could find her, offer her a road unfurling like a ribbon, a thick tangle of trees as far as she could see.

◊ ◊ ◊

The door to the orphanage was smaller than she remembered and opened silently. Sister Alice didn't recognize her at first, but then teary and apologetic, hugged her and Sebastian for a long time, then led her down the freshly painted hallway to a small room where Sister Francis sat propped up by pillows, shrunken to half her size.

"She's been ill," Sister Alice whispered. "But she's doing somewhat better now."

Michaela sat down with Sebastian on the edge of the bed. Sister Francis held her arms open, and Michaela hugged her gently, then carefully laid Sebastian in her arms. "Oh look at him," Sister Francis said, gently stroking his cheek, bending forward to kiss the top of his head. Sister Francis looked frail, but her beautiful, serene face was unchanged, the blue of her eyes like light shining off the ocean.

"I've missed you," Michaela whispered. Still holding Sebastian, Sister Francis gathered Michaela into her arms. Michaela wanted to tell her everything—if she couldn't tell Sister Francis, who would she tell? But what would be the words? *Such love. Too much love.*

It was on the drive home, back to her small empty rooms that the fear had risen from her belly, begun to spread into every limb. She had wanted to fly off the road, drive onto the lip of rock overhanging a field of tall grass and continue high into the air. It took all her strength to keep the car going forward, to stop her hands from turning the wheel suddenly and sharply. When she turned her key in the apartment lock, her hands were shaking. When she tried to rock Sebastian to sleep, he fussed and cried against the irregular pounding of her heart.

The next day, she woke in the grip of a terrible fear. She couldn't stop imagining one awful thing after another happening to Sebastian. Sebastian hurt as a car hurtled into hers, Sebastian falling from his crib onto the hard floor, Sebastian slipping in his bath, remaining under water too long before she could reach him. She tried to keep busy to distract herself, but all day, her heart kept pounding. The next day, it was no better.

Now, two weeks since it began, she can barely eat or sleep. Each night that she rocks in her chair, awake long into the night, she tells herself that tomorrow she will do more than feed Sebastian, walk through the streets of the city. She'll begin to look for a place to teach, buy more food, put a sheet on the bed. But each night her sleep is inhabited by terrifying dreams.

One day she can't get out of bed. She pulls the covers over her face. She hears Sebastian crying, and though she knows what she needs to do, she can't move. Her legs refuse to budge, her body is no longer subject to her will. It is hours before she can drag herself up, and when she does, Sebastian is asleep, exhausted from crying. She paces back and forth by his crib, waiting for him to wake up.

The rest of the day, she keeps moving. She walks up and down the city, Sebastian strapped to her. She is afraid to go home, afraid that if she falls asleep, once again, she won't be able to get up. When it finally grows dark, she drags herself inside, feeds Sebastian dinner, and collapses with him on her bed.

The next morning, it's there, lying beside her, the knowledge of what she must do. She wants to wrestle with it like Jacob wrestled with the angel, but it is stronger than she is, this terrible certainty. Still, for hours, she doesn't move.

But in the afternoon, she bundles Sebastian in a few layers. Fills two bottles with milk. She looks at his sleeping face, lifts him gently into her arms. She closes the door behind her. Walks down the bare metal stairs, then steps out onto the bustling street.

A calm has taken over, a quiet hum as she walks, another person in the throngs of people absorbed into the breath of the city.

Her arms know what they're about to do, but still her mind denies it.

She sees a church. Its steps are too cold. Dirty scraps of newspapers lift in the wind and settle. Two nuns are parking an old, gray Chevrolet in front of the church, then one of them feeds coins into the meter. She is diminutive, and from the back, reminds her of Sister Francis. They leave the doors to the station wagon unlocked, walk up the stairs and into the church. Michaela opens the door to the car and places Sebastian carefully on the passenger seat.

She is crying now and when she bends down to kiss him, his features grow soft and blurred.

Is this what it felt like?

She opens the window closest to him a crack and then gently closes the car door.

When she was leaving the orphanage, Sister Francis had handed her a small packet of things. An old rosary she never removed now from her coat pocket, its beads which had known Sister Francis's every wish, every prayer. But also, a letter dated May 15, 1974, the day she'd turned seven, the last day she'd seen her mother.

> *My dear Michaela, my blossom that I dropped. I am so so sorry. Let yourself drink the love the sisters have for you. Let yourself know that it wasn't for lack of will—*
> > *That I can barely keep myself up and moving forward.*
> > *Would that I could have fashioned you a stronger mother.*

Michaela crosses the street and stands leaning against a lamppost with the last of her strength.

She closes her eyes to keep out the words, but they are coming.

> *When your father left when you were still a baby, it was only then that I discovered the thinness of my skin, the muscles that were missing, the voices, the demons that peopled my dreams.*
> > *Some of us just can't do it.*
> > *It was to keep you safe.*

From across the street, where she is standing beside a lamppost, she sees the door to the church open. She knows that they will offer him their silence, their god, their love but that he will always search them for her face. That in the end, his veins will run with grief.

She wants to run across the street but she can't.

The door to the church opens again, and this time, the nun that had reminded her of Sister Frances emerges and makes her way down the stairs. Michaela watches as she steps onto the pavement, looks at her watch, walks around to the driver's side and opens the car door. She freezes, then almost falls backward in fright. She grips the car door with one hand as she stares at Sebastian. She crosses herself quickly then runs to the passenger side, opens the door, lifts Sebastian into her arms.

Did you see, mother, the way they glanced upward?

Did you feel your cells gathering in warning, threatening to storm?

Were you able to breathe mother? How in the world did you breathe?

Michaela turns and begins to walk away, one leaden step after another.

Then the sidewalk gives way. Tree branches loom close to her face. A chorus of voices is rising all around her as if the whole world were trying to talk to her at once.

Michaela—she can just make out her mother's voice above the din, though it's softer than she's ever heard.

Michaela, my love.

She drinks the voice in like milk.

Some of us just can't do it.
Let me look at you.
There there.

Anya's Angel

My mother once told me that the way she understood it, we were living in the only existing physical universe, which was but the palest reflection of the many non-physical universes that existed. That there was, however, a throughflow between the worlds, and just as some spirits and acts of the divine trickled down to us, so did our actions affect the other layers of worlds.

It was late when she said this, past midnight. She was sitting in the kitchen, a notebook in front of her. She had decided to study kabbalah. She couldn't talk to my father about these things. He had built a reputation on his agnosticism and his particular bent had grown a name, had turned his name into a noun. So when I would come upon my mother in the kitchen at all hours of the night, her glasses sliding down her nose, the books open before her, it was like coming upon her in an affair, only worse; a body is much more easily disengaged than angels and demigods and the remnants of worlds that now clung to her. I wondered if perhaps she was going to die, if she knew and was not telling us and needed to map out the realms into which she thought she might step. I wondered if perhaps it was to escape us, if we exhausted her—the constant stream of my father's scholarship, my own incessant wanderings and returnings; if having been only partially alive by the side of my father for years, she was finally claiming a territory onto which he would not follow her.

As she moved away from us, she became gradually more alive, and I was caught in the ironic moment of knowing what she must have felt at the first signs of my unstoppable separation and departure, the departure of her only son. Observing her at the kitchen table late at night with her books, her hair coming down out of a loose barrette, I felt that I had to let her go, that if I intimated that in any way I needed her to be the rock against which I was to kick off yet again, she would cast aside her books and I would have her grounding, her growing weightedness on my conscience.

So I held still and let her drift away. As did my father in his silent, impenetrable way, and she looked down at us, both accusing and relieved that we could have so little need of her, as if perhaps we had been tricking her all along, holding her hostage when in fact we could handle our own angst, navigate our own way in the world.

Sometimes I was tempted to draw close to her again and hide from my father's unceasing disapproval of me, of my lack of commitment to any discipline. Especially when he would emerge from his cave of a study, his tall frame bent from hours of hunching over a desk, when he would blink at us, remember slowly who we were, then launch into a lecture perfect in its logic, flawless in its arguments about how I was wasting my life, how in doing so many things, I was actually doing nothing.

"It is an illusion, Adam," he would say, "that one can in this way acquire wisdom, acquire any kind of universal perspective. If you truly want to understand, to know, to be able to see, choose one discipline and master it. In it the entire universe will be reflected."

These were the moments when I wanted to side with my mother, stand in her growing light and say something to my father about travel being the key to my soul's work. But ultimately I couldn't, because I wanted no part at this time in my life in discourses on soul sparks and states of consciousness. I had been surrounded for too many years with lofty and cerebral endeavors, and it had left me with a corporeal hunger, with a desire for landscapes of mountains and water, for rocks carving the bare soles of my feet, for bodies entangled in mine.

And so for three years now I'd been traveling. I couldn't get enough of fields racing by the windows of trains, of mountains red, pale, hung with clouds or swallowing whole enormous suns. There was knowledge that suddenly became tangible in the leavings, the departures, in the pulse of a rushing train. It was clear to me at times that therein lay access to true wealth and to the most important knowledge, which was silent and inarticulate.

Anya knew it, as we sat on the train up to Machu Picchu, her head on my shoulder, a thick striped blanket we'd bought in a local market draped over both of us. Anya knew this and so much more.

✿ ✿ ✿

Between my various journeys, I would usually come back to New York, and, because my stays were brief and often centered around the need to earn money for the next trip, I would stay in the large Riverside Drive apartment my parents had purchased near Columbia so that my father could move easily between his home study and his office. As much as he could manage to, he avoided Broadway with its teeming life, walked up Riverside instead, then cut to West End until he was thrust onto Broadway and into the world. Then he would hurry—I had seen him do this—looking neither left nor right until the gates of the university swallowed him and he headed to the safety of his office. He had grown, lecture by lecture, paper by paper, post by post, with bits of my mother's life blood stuck to him at every step, into the eminent biblical critic of his generation, as erudite and dry as the parchments he studied, as the urns and manuscripts he flew all over the world to see. He had translated and analyzed one of the alleged authors of the Old Testament, had, it would almost seem sometimes from the way he spoke, sired him, and in the process, abandoned me in his favor. How could I compete with long tractates on the vestments of priests, the charred remains of temple offerings, the purple linen, the cedar, the silver? This son of my father's constructed for him the world he most wanted to see, allowed him to imagine taking into his hands ancient goblets and candelabras, recited for him centuries of genealogies.

Until her recent venture into the very mysteries that my father sought to dissect, my mother had eased her own loneliness by reading incessantly, anticipating the trips they would take, and throwing dinner parties for my father's circle of colleagues. To many of their generation, she seemed the quintessential academic wife. Bright and articulate, she had given up pursuing her own Fulbright in Semitic Languages to marry my father and move with him from one post-doctoral position to another until he was tenured at Columbia. She was respected and even loved in the circles in which they moved. But when I would see her at these parties, a drink in her hand, her faraway expression, it was so clear to me that hers was a life unfulfilled. Her stifled wanderlust was apparent in the way she dressed, in the Moroccan and Tunisian gowns and dangling earrings she wore, which she'd found in various North African markets, in the way she had filled the living room with the treasures she had picked up. Watching her move across that large room that held, along with its conventional sofas, antique Persian copper trays, and walls hung with Tibetan masks and Spanish ceramic plates which conquered every remaining bit of space, I thought: I am living out her unspent passion. Of course I was no less predictable where my father was concerned. Son of the eminent scholar, with no academic aspirations, having never held down a respectable job, I knew at every turn that I had disappointed him.

Their friends oddly enough adored me—especially the wives. Their own children had marched passionately or willingly into careers in academia, or medicine, or science, all of which were respected in this world as long as one was in the forefront of research. I was the local renegade, the gypsy, and the wives in particular—though they never would have overtly encouraged this for their own children—seemed to goad me on.

It was on one of my brief jaunts home, as I was counting the days until Anya's arrival, that I had encountered my mother studying the mystical texts. I was waiting tables at a restaurant on Columbus Avenue and would return at two or three in the morning to find her at the kitchen table thumbing through huge books worn with use, their Hebrew letters curling and dancing their mysterious secrets across the page. Sometimes I would join her, draw her into a conversation about this or that, but usually I just kissed her, shut my door and lay on my childhood bed, my body exhausted, my mind alive with thoughts of Anya, as I remembered the stakes of our entanglement, then the return of calm as I forced myself to remember, instead, the sun coming up over Cuzco, Anya's hair on the pillow.

✿ ✿ ✿

I had met Anya on the outskirts of Cuzco where I had rented a house for a few months. I was outside fixing a broken shutter when she walked by, an unexpected vision in this Inca memory of a city. She was tall and pale and thin and could have been mistaken for Russian nobility at a different time. She said hello as if I didn't surprise her, as if she'd been encountering versions of me all her life. I invited her in for coffee and knew in the first few moments after she'd entered my house that I would fall in love with her.

We were sitting at my kitchen table, between us a large window with its view of the mountains above the red-tiled roofs of the city. I asked her how long she'd been here, where she'd been before and she began to tell me that she'd been in Cuzco for about a month, and before that she had traveled through the Greek Islands. But in my mind, I was already kissing her lips, waking up next to her in the overcast morning, falling asleep with my head in her lap as we sped through the night on Andean trains.

I don't know what came over me but I took her hand and said, "This is going to sound weird—but I think we're going to travel together. Yes, really. You're going to travel with me. Japan, Isle of Man, Madagascar, you set the itinerary."

She laughed. "I'm not so sure."

"Seriously," I said. But she was frowning and made a motion as if to brush something away and without any introduction, she told me that she was dying. She had been diagnosed—she spoke quickly as if to get this speech behind her—approximately eighteen months before with a rare form of leukemia. It was currently in remission but the doctors had told her the next time it surfaced, that would be it. She had opted not to combat it again with aggressive treatments, but wanted instead to try and live this last stretch as fully as she possibly could. And so she'd been traveling, and where for years she had worked hard to juggle her two somewhat incompatible loves for archaeology and poetry, she was now devoting herself exclusively to the poetry. The archaeology though—she paused, then laughed—was not really allowing her to abandon it as increasingly her poems were describing particular places—their rituals, their many layers of time and civilizations.

She paused, looked out the window then slowly turned back to me.

"What about your family?" I asked, though somehow I already knew that there was no family in the picture.

"I was raised by my paternal grandparents," she answered. "My parents died in a car crash when I was very young. My grandparents just know that I'm traveling. I don't want them to know anything else yet."

I wanted to reach across the table, take her hand but I didn't. "Have you been traveling alone this whole time?"

"No." She looked away. "I was with someone for many years. Hans and I met on a dig. When I was diagnosed, he left his work to travel with me. We traveled through the Middle East, then the Greek Islands. We settled for a while in Santorini. But then I asked him to leave. I didn't want—I don't want to do that to anyone."

She stopped awkwardly and I stopped asking questions. We just sat there for a long while in silence looking out the window that held a view of the mountains coming alive with light as the sun dropped.

"Come," I said on an impulse. I grabbed a bottle of wine, some bread and cheese and led her out to the rocky hilltop a few yards from my house. I held out her glass and she took it, the wine dark and opaque. We clinked our glasses in a silent toast.

When she wanted to leave, I walked her to the small house she'd rented in the center of town. I had been in love before, been entangled in various relationships of more or less intensity, but never had I felt such a sharp sense of recognition. I understood for the first time the word *destiny* as if only now it had sprung open its ponderous door and I was entering it, the winding cave-like grotto that it was. Entering it with this woman whose spirit was so much larger and braver than mine. I touched her cheek, brushed some hair back from her face, asked her if she wanted me to stay.

"No," she said. "Is that okay?"

"Of course." I kissed her forehead. "Good night. I will come to see you tomorrow."

But in the middle of the night, there was a knock on my door and she was there. "Damn it," she said as she let me put my arms around her, as she buried her face in my chest.

She stayed with me that night and those hours held all of the complexities of what was to come—of bodies very much drawn to one another, then the long hours that followed in which I held her as one would hold a child. The intimacy of her sleep felt both precious and unbearable. She stayed with me the next night and the next and the next and with each day we spent together, it was more difficult to imagine how I would do it—let her go on living the way she'd chosen to live—and, when the time came, let her go.

We lived together for a couple of months in what was for me, and I think for Anya, one of the strangest and in many ways most extraordinary stretches of time I'd known. We lived both passionately and carefully. There was an economy in the way we dealt with everything. We spent our days separately. Anya avoided the hot stretches of the day, using those hours to write in the house she still kept in the center of town. She ventured out, first in the early morning hours when only the carts were stirring, and then later when the sun lowered behind the houses. She would walk for hours then, not wanting to miss the shift of light on the soft white walls of the buildings, the growing shadows, the lifting winds. We would meet in the evening, bring together food we had bought in the market and prepare a feast to take outside, often joined by children who lived nearby. With all their semblance of normalcy, those days and weeks demanded from me an enormous discipline. If I was to truly honor the path she'd decided to take, I couldn't break down and think about what was to come.

✿ ✿ ✿

Each day when she left the house, I pulled out my journal and wrote. Nothing profound—just descriptions of some of the mountain villages and sketches of daily life in Cuzco. But when I heard her coming, I hid my work. Partly because I didn't want in any way to encroach on a domain so preciously hers, but also—and perhaps this was more the point—having read some of her work, I felt like a complete novice, both in the writing itself and in the breadth of experiences I had to bring to the page.

Then one day—I hadn't been paying it much attention—I realized that my money was running out. Anya had enough to keep going but not enough for the two of us and I wouldn't allow her to waste any of it supporting me.

"Come to New York." I said. "It will take me just a short while to put some more money together."

"I don't want to get sick in New York."

She was leaning against me, her head on my shoulder. We were on the train, heading up to Machu Picchu. We took this ride at least once a week. I wasn't sure anymore whether it was that spectacular destination or the climb together high into the clouds that we preferred but it had become a ritual of sorts for whenever one of us needed some perspective. Indeed it was hard to imagine Anya in New York, or anywhere other than Cuzco. Still I couldn't imagine leaving her alone for long, and after some time I managed to convince her to join me. We contracted that I would leave in a few weeks and that she would follow several weeks later, once I'd had a chance to settle and find a job.

❋ ❋ ❋

Even after all the traveling I had done, the transition to life in New York was brutal. And, to make matters worse, I was growing increasingly uneasy about having asked Anya to come. With every day that I wandered through the city amidst the sea of faces hurrying I knew not where, hungry for things that I knew were meaningless to Anya, with every evening that I spent working in the restaurant amid the chatter and the mindlessness, with every night that I returned to the strangeness of my parents' household where it was impossible to ignore the chasm growing between them, I found myself wondering what I had done in imploring Anya to join me.

My father was emerging less and less from his study. He seemed to be working even harder, as if in nurturing the new youngsters in the department, he was being pursued by his own mortality and was determined to uncover yet another layer, yet another detail heretofore unknown.

As he continued to withdraw, my mother seemed that much more preoccupied. She would study her books late into the night. In the mornings she was often gone when I awoke. She would return apologetic and smiling, as if I had caught her at something. I found myself wondering if perhaps there could be someone else, but no, it violated everything I thought I knew of my mother.

But then one day, I happened to return from work in the early hours of morning and spotted her. I had run into an old friend at the restaurant, and after my shift we'd found a bar and talked until dawn. When I returned home a little before six, the building was still asleep. Only the doorman stirred briefly when he saw me. But as I entered the elevator to go upstairs, I suddenly saw my mother coming out of one of the downstairs apartments. I stepped out of the elevator only to see her turn back suddenly, as if she'd forgotten something, and knock on the door she'd just left. I moved a bit closer. The door opened. It was dark in the apartment behind her and I couldn't make out who she was talking to. It was none of my business, I told myself, but I was already coming up behind her, tapping her gently on the shoulder. She started, then turned. "Adam!"

Staring out at me was a very old man with a long white beard. He smiled at me over her shoulder. He was a small man, a cross between an elf and a rabbi. He must have been in his nineties. His eyes sparkled with life in great contrast to his body. His features exuded—I would say light if it didn't sound odd and magical but it was an almost impossible and unnatural kindness. My mother stepped back and introduced us. The old man nodded at me. I had the sense that he was assessing me in some way. I don't know what it was that he saw but he looked puzzled. My mother retrieved a book she'd left behind and rode up in the elevator without speaking. When we reached our door, she motioned that we should sit in the living room, far from where my father was asleep, and she began to tell me the story.

The man she'd been visiting was indeed a rabbi, originally from a part of Russia in which there once had been a large Jewish community. The local synagogue had organized people to take care of him until now, but at the moment there was no one. She would go and have tea with him early in the morning, straighten his apartment, make sure his bills got paid. He had introduced her to some kabbalistic ideas and that's what had gotten her intrigued. He didn't think it was a good idea to delve into it without a strong basis in Jewish learning. In fact, he thought it could be dangerous, but she was intrigued and had insisted.

"Where's his family?"

She looked away.

"Well, I don't have to tell you about the roundups that took place in the small villages and shtetls, the pits, the mass graves."

She paused.

"His whole family was killed in one of those."

"How did he manage to escape?"

"He happened to be in the States raising money for an orphanage he had just established. He wanted to go back and see if he could save any of his remaining family, but his relatives here forbade him to go, told him there was nothing he could do, that if he went he was sure to die too. Anyway, according to some of the villagers who witnessed it, right after the group of people that included his parents, wife and children were marched out to the forest and killed, it started to storm, thunder and lightning and torrential rains. The soldiers who had carried this out didn't even bother to fill in the pit but left to return to their barracks. It later reached him that one of the villagers had seen a little girl who matched the description of his youngest child, crawling out of the pit and running into the forest. He spent years after the war trying to locate her but to no avail."

My mother began to cry. I sat there imagining that I saw that child, digging her way up through twisted limbs, climbing out of that human pile and into the forest and just running, running.

※ ※ ※

The next day the doorbell rang. It was the rabbi looking for my mother.

"She's not here," I told him. I asked him if he would like to come in for tea.

"No thank you," he answered softly with a strong Yiddish accent. My father stepped out of his study. The two men looked at one another. Then the rabbi turned to leave. My father must have seen just a religious old man—who symbolized for him a threat to fact and logic, to the tangible, scholarly proof he had built his life around. I have no idea what the rabbi saw.

※ ※ ※

"He visits other worlds," my mother said the next day. She had returned from the small Cuban café on the corner and was sitting at the kitchen table, her eyeglasses half steamed by the *café con leche* she had taken to go. She herself made wonderful cups of coffee but when her wanderlust struck, she would do whatever she could to salvage the pleasures of traveling. Sometimes she'd go to the tiny Cuban place and sit and contemplate the faces and listen to the conversations around her. Other times, like today, she would order the coffee to go and sit at the kitchen table as if she were awaiting some bus or plane.

"What do you mean?" I asked her.

She looked over her shoulder as if to make sure that my father wasn't approaching.

"He tells me that as he has gotten older, he has begun to visit other dimensions. He says that he has 'seen' all the souls of the members of his family but cannot find that one daughter. If she were alive, she would be middle aged by now, probably have grown children of her own. Why are you looking at me like that?"

"Are you going to go and look for her?"

"I don't know." She looked away. So she had at least considered it.

"He looked for years. There are agencies devoted to these searches—no, I don't think that I could do anything that hasn't been done."

"What do you think about all this?" I asked my father later that day. I knew even as I stood there that this was the wrong thing to do. It felt like a profound betrayal of my mother. Was I so desperate to find even the smallest common ground with this man that I would sacrifice my understanding of my mother? Was I so in need of his approval that I would betray that deeper certainty that her interest in all this comprised, more than anything, the beginning of her own independent journey? That she was spinning away from him and that he was oblivious?

"What I think," he began, "is that ultimately we are biological animals. The so-called spiritual hungers that individuals and groups have felt and expressed over the ages have served a very clear function for survival."

For once I was grateful for the intellectual sun that ruled this man, that he had not kindly or unkindly joined me in questioning my mother's judgment.

✿ ✿ ✿

New York was beginning to depress me. I went down to the Village to hear some jazz, wandered in and out of various neighborhoods in search of something. But nothing moved me. Nothing left a mark.

Then the day I was both anticipating and dreading finally arrived. Anya's flight was landing early in the morning. I went to pick her up in my father's old Volvo. She was thinner than I remembered. We held each other for a long time. I could feel the bones of her back, of her hip. She didn't need to tell me that the cancer was back. For the first time, she seemed fragile. We were silent in the car. She put her head on my shoulder and sighed. I looked out the window. I wanted to be driving by something beautiful, to show her from the first moment that there was something that I could offer her here, but there was nothing but drab highway, the wasteland of a strip mall, a housing project coming up on the right.

"I enjoyed your letters and the one from your mother. She sounds lovely," she said. "I'm excited to meet her."

"Perhaps I can ask her to lend us some money and we can go back a bit sooner."

She looked at me, surprised. "I thought you made it a point to always do this independently, to never ask them or anyone else for money."

"That's true," I said. "But it doesn't feel right suddenly to have taken you from Cuzco."

"Can we stop please?" she said suddenly.

"Stop where?"

"Anywhere. It doesn't matter. Just stop."

I pulled over to the side of the highway. Cars were hurtling dangerously by us.

"Look Adam," she said, "some things have changed since you left Cuzco and I need to know whether or not you are going to be able to change with them. It's true that I tried as long as possible to do as much as I could but I don't want to escape it anymore. What I realized after you'd gone was that by letting you in I had already made a choice—a choice I hadn't been ready to make with Hans—to accept your care and support, knowing what awaits you. This is a responsibility that I didn't want to take, that I didn't want to give to anyone. But it happened."

She looked away from me, out the window past the buildings, past the highway and trees.

"What I need now is to be accompanied, not rushed past this as if it weren't happening. I don't know what I am going to feel in the time ahead. I don't know what it will be like. All I know is that I want someone to help me look it in the face, help me perhaps make some sense of it. And it doesn't matter if it's in New York or Cuzco or Paris."

I nodded. I couldn't speak. I pulled back onto the highway, took her hand, held it all the way to my parents' house. I will never again be able to drive that stretch without reexperiencing those moments. It was as if we had entered a weather system. As if from that point on, the air grew thick with souls. I will always remember how each turn in the road brought a turn in my conviction—that I could do it—that I would fail—that I would falter as I was faltering now.

My mother hugged Anya as if she'd always known her. The table was filled with a rich assortment of cakes she had picked up at the Hungarian Pastry Shop. My father also greeted her warmly then began asking her all about Cuzco—questions he had for some reason never directed to me. I saw her face softening. I saw the bounty of my mother's love. I saw my father, and this was the strangest part, engaged in conversation with her as if she were someone of interest. He was asking her about the digs she had worked on and as she answered him, it emerged that she had worked on an important dig in Syria that had unearthed some biblical pottery. He grew animated in a way I had never seen. As Anya answered him excitedly, I began to relax. Perhaps this household could give her what she needed. When the doorbell rang, I wondered who it might be. It was an unlikely hour for visitors. Perhaps the rabbi, I thought, but then no, he had never come back since that day he had encountered my father. But when I opened the door, it was the rabbi.

"Who is it?" my mother called from the kitchen.

Before I could respond, she was turning the bend into the living room with Anya right behind her. I saw Anya stop short as soon as she saw him. I looked at the rabbi. He was riveted to her face. I saw pain and recognition and joy. Then suddenly, his eyes dimmed and he slumped to the floor. My father rushed in and together we pulled him to the couch, propped some pillows under his head. My mother ran to the kitchen and returned with some strong chemical, waved it under his nose.

When he came to, he couldn't take his eyes off of Anya.

"What is your name?" he whispered.

"Anya Vasileva."

"And your mother's name?"

"Tatiana."

"Tatiana? No your mother's name was Malkah. And what happened to your mother?" His voice was almost a whisper.

Anya's eyes grew teary. "She died in a car accident when I was three."

His brow furrowed.

I looked over at my father. It was impossible, as always, to read his expression.

The rabbi closed his eyes. Anya was beginning to tremble. I wanted to reach out and hold her but she shot me a look that said—no—not in front of him. I found myself suddenly wanting my father's cool, cerebral rationality. I wanted an intellectual refrain running through my head to diffuse what was unfolding before me.

The rabbi extended his arms as if reaching for Anya and without any shyness, she bent down to embrace him. It was impossible, I knew. Anya was not Jewish. Her family was Russian Orthodox. And she was too young to be his daughter. My mother turned to me as if she'd read my thoughts, as if we were thinking in unison, and whispered, "Perhaps his granddaughter?"

⚙ ⚙ ⚙

"It's impossible, "I told my parents later that night when Anya had collapsed into an exhausted sleep and the rabbi, exhausted too, having sat in our kitchen for hours drinking cup after cup of tea and holding onto Anya's hand, had, at my mother's coaxing finally fallen asleep on the couch.

"As far as I know, her parents . . ."

"Who knows? Who knows?" my mother interjected. "Perhaps that's why you ended up in Cuzco. Perhaps that has been the purpose of your travels—to find Anya, to bring her here."

"Hannah." My father looked angry. "Her parents were Russian Orthodox, not Jewish. Her last name has no known Jewish genealogy. Perhaps she bears some physical resemblance to his daughter. Perhaps he reacted that way because he wants more than anything, has been waiting perhaps, to close this chapter of his life."

"Perhaps," my mother said, retreating. "And perhaps it doesn't matter. If this will grant him even the illusion of family, if this will grant her the same . . ." Before she could finish her sentence, she stopped, came around the table and put her arms around me as if she had suddenly realized that I was about to lose Anya sooner than I had bargained for, that if this evening was any indication, this woman and this old man needed one another in some way that none of us could fully explain.

✿ ✿ ✿

And that was in fact the way it was. Anya began to spend a great deal of time with the rabbi. Sometimes I would accompany her to his apartment and he would welcome me. Still I felt that I was losing her. We had negotiated how we would handle what was ahead and I now had to wrestle with it in a new way. But when I saw him, when I saw the vastness of his presence, I thought, Anya is right to prefer him. What did I have to offer now?

I said that to her one night. "That's not true," she shot back. "That's just not true. It's that he's showing me something—There's something he has access to—I don't know how to explain it—hints, clues. When I'm with him I'm no longer afraid."

"You are beginning to sound like my mother."

I was the only one who seemed to be at a loss for a role. My father was growing close to her in a way that with every day surprised me more. She had shown him her poetry and its language which shifted from ancient to modern, its evocation of layers of civilizations had so excited him, he had taken a few of her poems to colleagues in both the Bible and Literature faculties and was on a crusade to have her work recognized and published. My mother was feeding her soups and stews and fresh pasta dishes, creating colorful and sumptuous displays of food that could only tempt, often talking with her long into the night, conversations which would hush when I approached. From the bits and pieces I overheard, there was nothing that I was not supposed to hear so much as that my presence reminded them briefly who they really were, how they were really connected. Without me they were a mother and her long lost daughter, catching up, telling their tales.

I spent my time fruitlessly trying to figure out whether Anya and the rabbi could possibly be related. According to my mother, the rabbi's family was from Kiev and Anya claimed that her father's family was from a small village thousands of kilometers away. I could find almost nothing that attached itself to Anya's mother's maiden name and she knew nothing of her maternal grandparents, only that her mother had been adopted. All of my research, dead ends.

The nights were growing increasingly difficult. Anya would come and lie by my side and I felt that this was all that was left me for me to do—to hold her until she fell asleep—then to lie with my eyes open lest the angel of death surprise us in our sleep.

✿ ✿ ✿

Then one day—I don't know what it was that called to me—I was sitting on the couch in the rabbi's small and dimly lit apartment. He and Anya were drinking schnapps and playing a game of chess by the light of a small table lamp. I was looking at her, at the line of her back, the thinness of her arms, the sudden lack of steadiness as she got up for a glass of water. I thought, she doesn't have much time, and whether or not this man was in any way family, there were other people who might want to see her.

"Anya," I said that night, "your grandparents—"

She nodded. "You can write to them, call them, whatever you like. And—" she hesitated.

"Who?" I asked.

"Hans—do you think you can find Hans?"

I didn't answer immediately. Then finally said, "Where is he?"

"Ouia, on Santorini."

At first I thought that I wouldn't, that I would allow myself perhaps that one act of selfishness. But when, with every day, I saw her energy flagging, I initiated a flurry of activity to find this Hans Uldrich, expatriate of Holland, citizen of Anya's heart. I contacted the Greek embassy which helped me track down a phone number for the municipality of Santorini.

We received a message back saying that Hans was on his way. I called Anya's grandparents in Chicago. Her grandmother started to cry when I told her Anya was with us. Hans had contacted them months ago when he was searching for her, had told them that she was ill. They'd been so worried and hadn't known where to find her. Anya's grandmother was recovering from a bad bout of flu but they would catch a flight as soon as they could.

Anya was declining rapidly. She barely had the strength to go downstairs. Instead the rabbi would come up to see her, set up a chess board next to her bed, teach her a few words in Yiddish. I would bring them cups of tea, sometimes just sit in a chair in the corner and read. One day as he was moving a pawn forward, I heard him say to her nonchalantly, smiling, "Chanale," which was what he called her, "I have seen Malkah, your mother. She is well."

With every day Anya's energy was dwindling. Thankfully, she was not in much pain but beginning to have trouble breathing. We would gather in the kitchen at night to debate what to do. Anya felt strongly about avoiding hospitalization. With the help of the doctor we had found for her when she had first arrived, we convinced her to agree to some oxygen. The rabbi now barely left her side. He held her hand, bent close to her and whispered things in her ear that none of us could hear. Her lips would curl up into a smile. I don't know if they were tales, bits of the past he believed they shared, or intimations of what was to come but she seemed to need him more than ever. We called Anya's grandparents, held the phone to her ear. I couldn't understand a word of the Russian but when the conversation ended, she was very upset. I took her into my arms, stroked her thin back, her hair, held her as she cried for the first time.

The doctor came again. It was clear from his expression when he emerged from her room that she was likely very close to the end. We increased the oxygen. I found myself hoping that she would hold on until her grandparents arrived, even until Hans arrived. At night, my mother would convince the rabbi to go and catch a little sleep and we would take turns sitting by her bedside. One night I must have dozed on my shift. When I woke, I remember looking at the clock; it was 4:44. I looked over at Anya. Her eyes were closed but I knew inexplicably that she was gone.

I lay my head on her chest and started to cry, at first silently, then louder and louder until I was wailing like a child. My mother rushed in, my father right behind her. She took me in her arms and held me. Then she led me out of the room and into the kitchen, where she switched on a small lamp and put up a pot of strong coffee. Outside the window, a thin yellow light was emerging from behind the dark buildings. The sounds of morning, of the city waking, were beginning to filter in through the open windows. I was sitting there, only intermittently aware of the light spreading through the room, of the tick of the large slate clock, unaware of anything but a gathering numbness, when the doorbell rang.

Hans was much the way I'd imagined him. The minute he saw our faces, he knew that Anya was gone. I led him to the bedroom and left him there alone. When he emerged, pale and barely meeting my eyes, I felt for this man who was grappling with his own shock and grief in a room full of people he didn't know. I led him up the back stairs to the roof. The sun was just coming up. I pulled out a cushion I kept hidden up there, put it on the highest perch and turned to go.

"Stay here as long as you like."

"Thanks," he said. I knew that whatever I felt about him, I was ultimately the one who had accompanied her this last stretch, that if I had wounds to address, his were no less deep.

✿ ✿ ✿

When Hans came down, my mother poured him some coffee. As he was beginning, at her insistence, to have a little something to eat, my mother jumped up.

"The rabbi—we must tell him."

She left to go downstairs and returned a few moments later with the rabbi. Hunched over and unabashedly crying, he nodded at us, then walked slowly on my mother's arm into Anya's room and remained there for a long while. Hans, my father and I were left in the kitchen. No one spoke. My father was drumming his fingers along the edge of the table. After a few moments he mumbled "excuse me," and got up and left. I heard the door to his study close. Hans's gaze was fixed out the window, his body turned away from me, tense. But still we sat together, as if she would have wanted this.

✿ ✿ ✿

I've been in Santorini for several weeks now. At first I thought that perhaps I should go somewhere else. But when Hans suggested that I come and spend a few weeks, it somehow felt right. I knew that Anya's grandparents would arrive in New

York and that my mother would make them welcome. I knew that in one form or another, at least temporarily, she was going to leave my father, and that this leaving would launch the next part of their lives. I knew all this and I did not want to be there. And so I accepted Hans's invitation and together we took the night flight to Athens, then slept on either side of a life boat on the crowded boat trip to Santorini. He found me a room on the outskirts of the village and we met in the evenings at one of the bars frequented mainly by villagers, but also by a few of his ex-pat friends.

I don't know exactly what I did with those days—sat and watched the sun on the water far below my daily perch, where the big tourist ship circled in search of the new port, and goats scampered up and down the rocky slopes. There were so many questions. An emptiness that had always been there now big enough to swallow me. And the strangeness of all the events— coincidence or not? And if not, how to explain it?

I had gone to see the rabbi several days after Anya died. I don't know what I'd intended to ask him, even if I'd intended to ask him anything, but I had a sudden desire to see him. When no one answered, I tried again but I knew even as I knocked louder and louder that he was gone, like a soul that had lost its interest in the world. I went to get my mother, then the land-lord. We found him on the couch. It looked like he had died in his sleep.

Hans and I were meeting in the evenings, a strange echo to my days with Anya. We would get together at one outdoor bar or another, and watch the sun erupting over the water, the white houses aglow. There was some ritual we were perform-ing here and for the time being, it seemed to be one we both needed. He asked me for stories of Anya those last months. I did not ask the same. But it was growing clear to me how little we have of someone. I had this piece. He had that piece. I coveted his piece and it was apparent, from the questions that he asked, from the expressions that crossed his face, that he coveted mine.

But with every day that I spent with Hans and with his circle of friends, the more I saw what I might become. I saw that he had not yet recovered from losing Anya, but also that he was keeping that pain alive, that it had become an excuse for some inability to move. I saw the people with whom he surrounded himself, each with his or her own life story, with his or her particular pain, looking to blur it in the Greek sun, in the sweltering bodies that poured in predictable waves out of Europe.

It was becoming clear to me, though I felt powerless yet to act on it, that traveling for traveling's sake would no longer fulfill me. That I would wander and sit and climb and drink with little or no satisfaction. That my life would feel purposeless. The people I would meet would seem to be running from themselves. Their stories would tire me. There were some things that I wanted to do. I wanted to finally take the various pieces I'd been writing from their secret place and see where they would go. I wanted to walk into my father's study and tell him what I had learned about the preciousness of time to accompany those we are connected to—how many years we had wasted, were wasting.

I was thinking about this one day on my ledge, watching the sunlight dancing on the water, the fishermen's boats going out with their frayed nets. Perhaps it was the particular cast of light, but I remembered one of my mother's discourses on the movement between worlds, on the way in which our every action created an angel, was reflected in a world of angels and suddenly, for the briefest second, I thought I felt something hovering just above my head. I thought I saw wings beating hard against the air, a face turned from me, tense with the tremendous effort it was taking to remain in one place. I didn't need to decide whether or not it was real. It didn't matter. What I knew was that very soon I would move on; very soon I'd be on the deck of a departing boat, with the spray and the circling gulls, all of me in one single, plaintive ache for Anya as I watched this volcanic rock of an island recede into the glimmering sea.

Into the Atacama

*T**he Chilean desert, which runs 4,300 kilome-*
ters from the southernmost point of Tierra del Fuego to its border
with Peru, is the driest desert on earth. It encapsulates within its
narrow girth between Andean ridges and the Pacific, a good deal of
Chile's tumultuous history—its copper and nitrate economy, its his-
tory of colonial exploitation, and even a few stories of Nazi chases.
Laboring through it on the Pan American highway, or by its small
and dusty back roads, one cannot help but feel the relentless wrestling
of man and the elements, especially when one witnesses the now life-
less towns and settlements that had once grown around the mines
like devoted encampments around divine, life-giving temples.

Valle de La Luna, the forlorn remains of a now defunct saline
lake, glistens mysteriously at night, absorbing and reflecting the
secret migrations of the night sky, and has long been a magnet for
the continent's hippies and mystics. One can easily imagine scenes of
romance or life and death passion plays in that crumbling natural
amphitheater created by salt and light.

Restless Nomad Traveling Guides
Vol. 18: Chile

We are only two hours out of Santiago and I am tired of
smiling. The wife looks my way. Two hours of our husbands

exchanging stories in Spanish, laughing at jokes, at memories I cannot spy on, the wife and me in the back seat of the Benz, having exhausted my fifty words of Spanish and listening to her fewer words of English. We are both aware that we are trapped and helpless.

I shift my gaze to the landscape which is beginning to turn into desert. Dry and wild, it speeds by us—rocks, thin and thirsty bush—and it's only the beginning. We will be traveling with Lalo and Marlena for five days and four nights into the heart of the Atacama Desert and back.

My husband stares ahead. I have receded for him as he drinks in the long and rough torso of this part of his country. Takes in purple, then orange peaks, a terrain he used to travel through when he was young, his guitar resting beside him, a small bag of clothes in the back of the old, rattling car as he and the other members of his band headed with little plan or worry toward Bolivia or Peru. While I was still dutifully bringing home A's, and not so dutifully exploring the first wonders of sex in the back of large Brooklyn Cadillacs, my future husband was heading north or northeast where he would get swept up in crowds that became demonstrations, in coups that appeared and dispersed like sudden storms.

I steal a glance at the wife's long legs, at her lightly highlighted hair.

She had apparently married Lalo when she was just a girl to escape a family that had kept her tethered. I knew this from my husband, who was a childhood friend of theirs, part of the inner circle of a downtown middle-class Chilean upbringing which he too had inhabited with his first wife—his child bride—until he broke away and escaped out into the larger world.

Marlena, the wife, smiles at me. "You have in Boston good empleads?"

"Sorry, what?"

"Good—*cómo se dice empleadas?*"

"Maids," my husband translates, his voice in neutral so as not to betray the absurdity of the question in our particular circumstances, where we were each working forty hours a week to make the rent, while pursuing our "art" at night. He leaves that task to me.

"No, uh, we don't have any maids."

"No?" She looks embarrassed. "I have only two," she says, her voice trailing off.

"Is it a problem, getting good maids in Chile?"

"*Sí,*" she says, looking at her feet.

The car has grown silent. Lalo puts on a CD—the one we have brought him as a gift, *Making Music,* with Zakkir Hussain on tabla and Jan Garbarek on sax. The darting, breathless improvisation on Indian themes fills the awkward silence, causes the mountains rushing by on either side to suddenly loom ancient and primordial.

"How are you, lovely *gringa?*" Lalo turns to me as he approaches a narrow curve, one hand on the wheel.

"Fine," I say. There will be time to find out if I can say what I really think. But right now in this speeding car, the territory within warrants as much observing as the one without.

It is night when we reach Los Villos.

We say goodnight and go to our separate bungalows. My husband has brought his guitar but is too tired to play. I lie awake for hours, listening to the sea.

The next morning we wander around the town. Los Villos, I learn, is a resort for Chileans who stop short of venturing into the real desert, into the *Norte Chico* which begins here, and then the endless *Norte Grande* with its barren stretches, its pocked surface where the mines that fed this country used to be. Lalo,

Marlena, and my husband do not seem interested in the town. For them, it is simply a starting gate because these crowds are not their crowds, not their class, though they would never say it. I am curious about everything, including how different strata of Chileans vacation, what they wear, what they eat. But the others are eager to move on and we climb into the car and plow northward.

✧ ✧ ✧

The desert dissolves into the horizon like the end of the earth itself. After a long stretch of driving, we pull into Guanaqueros for lunch. The town is small and offers itself slightly bruised and tired, but sweet too, and newly painted for summer travelers.

There is a church in the center of town, and next to it a plaza of trees and benches on which no one sits. This is another Chile from the one represented by the European boutiques in Providencia that my sister-in-law had proudly shown me, or by the new mall in the northern suburbs of Santiago that boasts having nothing native. As if that version could erase this modest square, the women whose thighs had widened with each child they'd carried. The men in hats from the 1950s peering out of dark doorways. The tiny shops selling candy, gum, homemade sweets. A Coca-Cola T-shirt billows in the wind from the doorway of a shop next to some graffiti that reads "Yanqui go home."

After lunch, we wander around the town. "Stand in front of the church," Lalo says, snapping a picture of me. Draped in a long skirt and my comfortable traveling tunic, my hair wet from a morning shower, I was smiling at my husband, probably out of relief at being out of the car. Later, in Santiago, when I developed the picture, I looked small and insignificant, the church spire rising behind my head like a mountain peak.

✧ ✧ ✧

Lalo turns his head to look at me just before another hairpin turn.

"So *gringa*," he says, "you are Jewish."

"Yes," I say, not knowing what's coming.

He takes the turn at high speed, then slows uncharacteristically to let one of the many trucks that prowl the Pan American Highway go by us on the left.

"Maybe you can explain to me why you people stay so closed and how you always manage to make so much money."

I look at my husband to see if he will rally but his eyes are peeled forward. No, I think, I'm just not going to answer him.

"I don't know, Lalo," I say.

"Hey *huevón*," he says to my husband, "have you heard this one? A Jewish man and his son are leaving Europe for America. After a few hours, the son says, 'Daddy, couldn't we just buy a ticket for the boat,' to which the father replies, 'Shut up and keep swimming.'"

My husband chuckles.

Lalo launches into what I make out to be a few more Jewish jokes at which everyone laughs except for me. I look out the window. The fantasy I'd had of this trip, of my husband and me making our way northward accompanied by his childhood friends who would grant me another glimpse into his soul, is receding with the light that is slipping into the Pacific. No, my husband—with whom I thought I'd traveled this distance as an ally—was fast becoming part of the strange and foreign landscape, slipping, after fourteen years of absence, into the old humor and mores of his *patria*.

◊ ◊ ◊

On this trip, I have suddenly become very Jewish. More Jewish than I have ever felt. Within an hour of our arrival to the family home, my mother-in-law, tiny and elegantly dressed, was emerging only sporadically from the kitchen behind me, and thus, without my full knowledge, observing as much of me as she could. She had the table brimming with *empanadas*, a salad of curled celery and olives, tomatoes and onions cut paper thin, a plate of *humitas*, their steam rising—a second round of pisco sours mixed and poured. My husband's Aunt Graciela, who had hoarded years of English from her decade of tutoring the British Ambassador's children, and who now sat across from me, her dark hair newly coiffed, returned her glass soberly to the table, looked me in the eyes, and said, "We hear that you are Jewish."

"Yes."

"What do the Jews believe?" she asked, wasting no time.

I tried to think quickly. What was she really asking? "Well, they believe in one god."

"And do they believe in Jesus?"

"That he lived at that time and broke away from traditional Judaism, yes. That he was the son of God, no."

I saw her catch her breath.

"And do you believe in the Trinity?"

"No," I said a little more quietly.

"And the Virgin?" she asked, almost breathless.

"No."

There was a silence as my mother-in-law came in and laid a huge platter of ham and cheese on the table, just in front of me.

"And do you want to have children?" Graciela asked. My mother-in-law looked like she just might cry.

"Yes," I said, and there was a practically audible sigh.

"*Gracias a Dios*," my mother-in-law whispered.

"*Salud*," my husband said, lifting his glass.

"*Salud mi hijita*," said Graciela clinking my glass.

◊ ◊ ◊

A few days later, my mother-in-law was sitting across from me at the breakfast table. She had prepared a plate brimming with fresh *marraquetas* and *hallullas* and poured us tea, smiling guardedly. As my husband and I chatted in English over where we might go that day, she read, from front to back, the morning edition of *El Mercurio*. When she reached the editorial page, I saw in one of the headlines the word "*Judíos*." The Pope was about to pay a visit and so the paper was summarizing some aspects of Vatican II. The headline, my husband translated, said that the Pope conceded in the early sixties that the Jews were not guilty of killing Christ. Had the news only just reached Chile? My mother-in-law looked across the table at me with relief.

My beautiful mother, in her late eighties and fading now like light at the end of a day, had warned me to always keep a low profile about being Jewish. It wasn't hard as an adult to understand why. It was her Aryan looks that had kept her alive. Her beautiful face, her flawless Polish, her ability to disappear into a crowd.

At first I had followed her lead. But by 18, I was defiant. I wore a Jewish star, which drove her mad; went off and spent two years after college in Jerusalem; and then returned confused, graduate school luring me back into the broader world in which she had always wanted me to lose myself. Her relief was palpable when I married a man so foreign to our tribe. "You will have," she had said, "another country to go to should it ever be necessary."

"Didn't Chile harbor Nazis?" I asked her.

"Not like some of the other countries," she replied. "You could hide should you ever need to. It's a long country."

✧ ✧ ✧

She was certainly right about the length. I am beginning to think that there's no end to this desert. It is the third day and after miles and miles of flat and gravely terrain where no bird lifts, no life stirs, after one thin and dusty town after another that looks as if the miners had only just departed, suddenly to the right of us, an abandoned train station circa 1850. We race past it in a blur. Then another stretch of scraggly bush and parched ground, then "Stop," I say. "Stop, please."

My husband turns to look at me.

"Look." I point to the extraordinary sight to our right. A huge and sprawling complex, rows and rows of roofless structures, the ochre and sand color of the desert, holes gaping where windows used to be.

"What is that?"

"A mining camp. Probably from the 1920s."

"Can we go see it?"

Lalo looks at his watch. "We have dinner reservations at nine o'clock."

"Dinner reservations?" I look around us. Flat dry land stretched in every direction. The very phrase seems so funny, I laugh. My husband frowns.

"All right, *gringa*. You want to see how we prostituted ourselves before your country and others? Come."

He pulls off the highway, we get out of the car and follow a rocky path that leads us down to the old mining camp. I begin to walk down the long aisles that separate the rows of connected "houses." Behind me Lalo is saying, "and here was a luxurious three-bedroom." I walk up and down the rows, peering into the rock-strewn enclosures that had once been rooms for the *salitre* miners and their families. When I get to the last row, I see a path leading to a low, drooping fence. Within the fence, half-buried by sand and rock, is a cemetery, the dusty tombstones leaning in every direction. At the far end of the cemetery where the last tombstones give way to the endless desert beyond, what looks like a bright colored cloth flutters in the wind.

It is red and it's sticking out of a small, half-broken box, which I realize is a coffin. The winds have swept the earth from the grave but the small coffin appears to have risen from the ground, like a reproach. The piece of cloth, which could have been a part of a shirt or a bandana, billows in the late afternoon wind, furling and unfurling like a flag.

I peer inside to see the small partly decomposed body of a child, covered in dull and dusty clothes. I sit down next to it, put my head in my hands and start to cry. There is a small stone lying on its side next to the grave. *Pablo Medina Alvarez,* it says. For two years now I had been struggling with infertility—tests, vials, calculations, sperm in a centrifuge—and my husband's reluctance to adopt. And this little boy, maybe two, maybe three, had arrived, lived, and so quickly died in this barren place. I hear Marlena's footsteps behind me. She crouches down next to me and puts her arm around me. After a few moments, she gets up and peers into the coffin, then quickly turns aside and throws up. And I know then—though of course there could have been another, more obvious explanation—that she is pregnant.

We drive in silence to Antofagasta. My husband is many shores away. My belly is aching its strange, deserted ache. I suspect that Marlena knows that I am not managing to get pregnant, and that it is this unspeakable truth, more than all of her maids, and her husband's wealth and privilege, that has succeeded in driving a final wedge of silence between us.

✿ ✿ ✿

Antofagasta was once the main commercial gateway for shipping the bounty of Chile's great copper mines, and when we enter its streets, it is bustling with all the self-importance that comes with being a major port and the Atacama's largest city. Lalo drives through the crowded streets until we leave the city's center behind and drive down a quiet stretch where the water laps at the small sliver of land between the road and the sea, and unpretentious and festively lit seafood restaurants adorn the shore. A number of large boats are approaching the docks and when I inquire about them, Lalo explains that they deliver basic commodities that are scarce up here in the desert, then return with crates of *locos, congrio, machas*. We pull up to a restaurant that seems a bit tonier than the others and wait on the wicker chairs and lounges set up outside as the waiters scurry and apologize for having lost our reservation. Lalo speaks to them imperiously, a man used to getting his way, and I cringe at the obsequious apologies of the waiters, of the maître d' who all but bows to Lalo, a man he clearly does not want to disappoint.

A few minutes later, we're standing up to greet Lalo's sister, Estela, her husband, Tomás, and Tito, Marlena and Lalo's nineteen-year-old son, who is taking a course up here in the north, and staying with his aunt and uncle. They approach as fast as they can manage, with Tomás leaning on Estela and Tito and dragging his right leg.

I know from my husband that Tomás, a marine biologist here in the north, has just suffered a stroke and that before this happened, Estela was about to leave him. As they come up to us, Lalo introduces me and we kiss Chilean style.

Tito grins at me, clearly glad to see us. Tito is almost family. He lived with us for six months when he first came to study in Boston. He hugs his parents. Then we embrace.

"How are you?" he asks, then hugs me again. When he stayed with us, the two of us had grown quite close.

My husband comes up and embraces him, then tentatively puts his arm around me.

The waiters are pushing three tables together, lowering a white starched tablecloth. They hold our chairs until we are all seated. They sprinkle the table with bread and *aji*, tomato and onion salads. They pour us wine. Tomás and I are seated next to one another. His green eyes and sandy brown hair do not look Chilean. British, perhaps, I think.

Tomás's wife is on his other side. Delicately, inconspicuously, she tears his bread into bite-sized pieces like a child's, halves the thin slices of tomato and onion that make up his *Ensalada a la Chilena*, then she turns and begins to chat with Marlena.

Later I will try unsuccessfully to remember how the conversation began, how it was that Tomás and I eased into each other's presence. But right now, I am fully aware of every detail: the wind lifting the edge of the tablecloth, the force field that seems to ignite as we take our seats.

Everyone must know, I thought. Everyone must feel the air humming.

There is a current between Tomás and me—a strong and instantaneous recognition, as if we'd known each other forever. It is—in the purest sense—love, if love were a magnetic pull, soul to soul.

I don't have to wonder if he feels the same. His voice lowers and offers itself just to me.

He gestures to the ocean, crashing and receding only yards from where we sit and begins to tell me about the research he was doing before his stroke—about the world living clandestinely beneath the surface of the water, and what they are discovering in the primordial heat of thermal vents. There's an urgency as if he needs to impart this knowledge, not academically, not factually, but as it really is for him—a poem. He describes how in the most brutal temperatures, they've found four-foot tube worms that cluster in thickets with red plumes swaying like tongues of fire, miniature lobsters called Galatheids, bright red baby vent crabs that will grow white as they mature, primitive bacteria that may hold the earliest clues to the beginning of life, that may give scientists a glimpse into life as it might exist in non-earth environments.

I squint into the darkness at the sea rising and spewing its foam just in front of us.

I tell him about those years in my early twenties when I lived in Jerusalem and would occasionally travel down to the beaches and coral reefs of Dahab and Ras Muhammed, on the Red Sea. I tell what I had heard about Blue Hole—a 200-foot drop off the coast of Dahab where more than a few divers were lured too deep and never made it back up.

Yes, of course, he has heard of it. He would like to go one day, he says, and we both fall silent.

"And Jerusalem," he asks, shaking his head briskly so as to move on from the awkward silence, "what is it really like?"

I tell him about the smell of honeysuckle in the untended gardens that offer up flowers, voluptuous, bursting, grass that reaches, snake-like upward, weaving quietly between people's quarrels and midday naps. I tell him about the Bougainvillea and Eucalyptus, about the sky scorched purple and the domes and spires and the shadows they cast in that light. I find myself telling him about the tunnel outside Jerusalem that I walked through waist-deep in water, one Arab boy in front of me with a candle and one behind as we followed the water into the once besieged city. I tell him about camping in the Sinai and how the Atacama was both reminiscent of that desert and wasn't.

⚙ ⚙ ⚙

Our food arrives. The waiter circles us with wine. When he leaves, we turn to each other again, impatient to continue. I am aware of the growing tension around us. Back home, our conversation would not have caused the slightest stir, but here, where women rarely venture beyond the orbit of their husbands, it is another matter.

Lalo and Marlena are watching us carefully, refilling their glasses with a vintage Concha y Toro wine. Only my husband doesn't look my way. I try and convince myself that it's because he is not concerned. Because he knows that I live for these moments. For these discoveries of people whose stories I want to hear, with whom I want to share my own. He can sense too, I think, in the way that partners can, that this is not sexual, or romantic. My husband knows that he and I are traveling separately. That he is bearing witness to the ways in which his country has changed, the ways in which it has stayed the same. He is suspended between many parts of himself here. Later, it might all be assimilated or not, but for now, he is caught up in the many layers of his own history. And he has left me on my own, to find my own way in this barren place.

Lalo and Marlena are not so sanguine. They don't know me. Even from a distance they seem to be hovering. Then Lalo saunters over. He is a bit drunk. "So beautiful *gringa*, are you sure about what you are doing with my friend?"

"No," I say, "but I like to live dangerously."

⚙ ⚙ ⚙

When I next look up, dinner is done. The others have wandered down to the dock. Only Tomás, Tito and I are left at the table. Tito has headphones on and his eyes closed, and is nodding rhythmically to the music he hears. He opens his eyes for a moment and smiles as he catches me watching him.

"Can we walk down to the water?" Tomás asks.

"Of course," I say, and gently touch Tito's arm to get his attention.

Tomás leans on Tito and on me and puts most of his weight on his good leg as we hobble down to the water. We take off our shoes, Tito casually helping Tomás as if this were something he always did. The waves bound toward us, crash and dissolve, sending their soft spray to where we stand. The sand sucks at our feet as the tide recedes. I look at Tomás and then I know what I must do.

"Shall we?" I ask, gesturing toward the water. He laughs. "Yes," he says, "let's."

"Help me, Tito," I say, bending down and putting an arm behind Tomás's knees. He looks perplexed for a second then understands and together we lift Tomás into the cradle of our arms and begin to carry him into the water.

"*Hijo de puta,*" I hear Lalo yell from the dock, "*Qué locura!*"

I can feel my dress getting wetter and wetter and swirling around my legs. When we are deep enough, we lower Tomás into the water. After a few moments, he transfers his other arm from Tito to me and I am holding him in my arms like a child. The trust between us is the trust of centuries. Above us, millions of stars fan out and glisten, more stars than I have ever seen.

Lalo stands at the edge of the water, watching us, sipping a gin and tonic. Tito is grinning. I look past Lalo to where my husband sits in a beach chair, a glass of wine in his hand.

I understand that I am making things complicated for him. That I am asking him to take a stand here for my right to be who I am, to not play by the stiff Chilean social rules, to take a stand, though it would never be understood here, for who he's become. I also understand, from what I have seen of his country, that who he's become, in the years he's lived outside of his country, is miraculous.

Lalo comes up to the water's edge, signals that it's time to go.

We come out of the water, clothes stuck to us, chilled and laughing.

"*Fantástico, gringa,*" Lalo says, putting his arm around my shoulders. "You are going to keep us all on our toes."

Lalo hands Tomás some of his own dry clothes, and I take my bag from the car to find my own and go off to change. When we all return to where the cars are parked, I glance at Tomás, who is looking at me with a faint smile. I don't know whether I will see this man again. I don't know whether he will live. Estela has come to stand by his side. I hug him politely as all are watching.

"Send me something from Jerusalem the next time you go," he says.

I promise him that I will.

✿ ✿ ✿

We pile into the car. This time Marlena slips into the front seat and my husband gets into the back seat with me. Beyond this town, the desert will continue to unfurl for a good part of a continent. We are going to drive through the night to San Pedro de Atacama, watch the sun come up over Valle de la Luna, the one concession on this trip to the romantics we once were. But for now, my husband and I are as far from one another as the confines of the car will permit. The road reveals itself only for several feet at a time. Under cover of night, the Andes flirt and merge with the sky. There are no other cars in sight and the lights of Antofagasta are quickly lost.

After a while, Marlena turns and looks me in the eye. "The father of Tomás," she says, holding her hands to her shoulder as if holding a gun. She pulls the trigger.

"He was shot?"

"No no—he kill. He, *ay—cómo se dice en inglés?*" She takes a cocktail napkin from her bag, draws a swastika.

"He killed a Nazi?"

"No no—he—him" and she put her hand up in a heil salute.

"He was a Nazi?"

"*Bueno, eso lo que escuche,*" well, so I've heard, she says, and there is a faint smile on her lips as she attempts to reel me in to my husband, to my choices, to this journey on which I am a passenger.

No one speaks. For several hours, we travel in silence past the dark shadows of mountains, past hidden stretches of landscape. Despite the composure I am trying to maintain, I am shaken by Marlena's arrow. I am beginning to doubt everything. Was the connection I felt real? Or was Tomás also fascinated with finally meeting a Jew?

The road dips and we see a cluster of lights up ahead. Lalo slows the car.

"What do you think, *huevón?*" he says to my husband as a row of small bungalows comes into sight. "What do you say we stop for a couple of hours, hang out, sleep, and continue a little later?"

"Sure," my husband says.

Marlena and I are not consulted.

We pull up to a string of tiny thatched-roof structures. The proprietor, whom we have clearly woken, sullenly leads us to two small bungalows that are set back off the road. We have just closed our door when Lalo knocks.

"*Oye, huevón,*" he calls to my husband. "There's a pool table. Come and see."

My husband leaves without even meeting my eyes. I lie down on the bed. I am drifting off when I hear a knock on the door. It's Marlena.

"Are you sleeping?"

"No, come in."

"Ah, you have also mini-bar," she says walking up to a small refrigerator in the corner of the room that I hadn't even noticed. I get up and open it and laugh, finding it stacked with wine, beer and small cocktail bottles, nuts, candies, mineral water.

"What would you like?"

"Wine, if you have."

"Wine it is."

I pour myself a miniature Chivas.

I am halfway through my drink when I say, "Bastards, they are all bastards."

"*Hijos de puta,*" she says laughing.

"Infants," I say.

"*Animales,*" she adds.

She goes up to the refrigerator, takes some cheese and crackers. She puts some on a plate for me, then tosses me another Chivas.

We go back and forth, switching languages, trying out our invective against men.

"*Burros,*" I say in an attempt to say asses.

"Sticky," she responds.

"Sticky? Now you've got me. Do you mean slimy?"

"Yes," she says, bending over with laughter.

"Macho—" she continues, *cómo es la palabra*?

"Piglets," I say, and we begin to laugh so hard that we both need to pee. "You first," I say, gently pushing her toward the bathroom.

When she comes out, her face is pale. Within seconds, I know what has happened. I lead her over to the bed. Put my arms around her as she begins to cry into my shoulder.

"No, no, no."

"It doesn't necessarily mean it's over. Many women bleed. I'm sure Lalo can find the nearest doctor."

She is bending over, holding her stomach. I reach into my bag for some Motrin, pour her a glass of water.

"I'll go get Lalo," I say.

"It's not true," she whispers, grabbing my arm and looking me directly in the eyes.

"What's not true?"

"Tomás's father—a Nazi. He only think like Nazi."

"Don't worry about it," I say, and run out in the direction of the lit bungalow where I can see the two men angled over a long pool table.

My husband and I wait outside. After a while, Lalo comes out, looking pale himself. "She's okay," he says. "It's stopped for now. I will try to get her to sleep. I called Tomás and they will send a doctor first thing in the morning."

"Go," he says to my husband, handing him the car keys. "Go and catch the sunrise and come back. By that time, the doctor will have seen her and we'll start heading back to Santiago."

"No," my husband protests, "No, we'll we stay here."

"Don't be silly, *huevón*," Lalo says. "We came all this way. The *gringa* should see it. Go. There's nothing we can do until morning. We'll be waiting for you when you come back."

My husband reluctantly accepts the keys, opens the car door for me. For the first time, we will be alone for more than a few minutes. As soon as we leave the cluster of bungalows, we're surrounded by vast flat stretches, punctuated by the small dark shapes of desert scrub. In the distance, the huge, shadowed mountains. Nothing, I think, is what it seems here—a man so alive inside a numb body, a connection that perhaps I'd mistaken, graves that erupt from the ground. Maybe this marriage that I thought could stretch to accommodate my husband and me, separately and together, this bond that I thought would yield children, something larger than ourselves, is crumbling too. My husband puts on a Joan Manuel Serrat CD he finds in the car, and we each lose ourselves in our thoughts. If we speak, I know our words will fly in a thousand angry directions. So we hold back, until our silence winds before us like the dark, thin road, illuminated only by our headlights. We stop only once, at the entrance to San Pedro de Atacama, where we find a small restaurant that is still open. We share wine and empanadas, and still we barely speak.

When we finally arrive at Valle de La Luna, the ground is ecstatic, the moonlight dancing wildly off the crystals. The ground rises in strange, crusted shapes, then swirls downward as if it still held the memory of a whirlpool. The moon overhead is huge and full and the salt crystals glint and sparkle. While my husband searches for a place to sleep until sunrise, I climb the tallest crest of glistening rock I can find. The stars are fanned out above me in every direction. I feel something rising in me. An opening, slight and hopeful. I offer up a small prayer for Marlena's baby. I follow it with one for my own. My husband has found a small cove of flat rock, surrounded on three sides by pillars of rock and salt. He spreads a blanket on the ground, takes my hand, and in a tentative grasp that is itself a question, leads me to it.

I take him into my arms.

"I'm scared," he whispers into my hair.

"Don't be," I say, and offer him the press of my body as a compass, a map that may lead us back. All around us, the salt-encrusted earth is glistening. The full moon is playing with us so that as my husband starts to unbutton my shirt, slips his hands softly over my skin, for a moment that is as brief as it is exquisite, it seems to me that we are, in fact, on the same journey.